I WANT

For Annabel
Love from Maggie
for your
9TH Birthday!
xx

I want to be an
airline pilot

MARY WEEKS MILLARD

Best wishes,

May Weeks Millard

DERNIER PUBLISHING
Tonbridge

Text copyright © Mary Weeks Millard 2010
Illustration copyright © Alison Blackwell 2010
This edition copyright © Dernier Publishing 2010

First published 2010

Published by Dernier Publishing
P.O. Box 403, Tonbridge, TN9 9BJ, England
<www.dernierpublishing.com>

ISBN 978 0 9536963 5 2

Book design and production for the publisher by
Bookprint Creative Services, <www.bookprint.co.uk>
Printed in Great Britain.

To my beautiful grandchildren,
Jade, Danielle, Louise, Jason and Lisa Jane.
God loves each one of you so much,
and so do I!

Acknowledgements

My grateful thanks to my ever patient husband for all his encouragement. Also to Janet Evans of Dernier Publishing for all her advice and work in the production of this book.

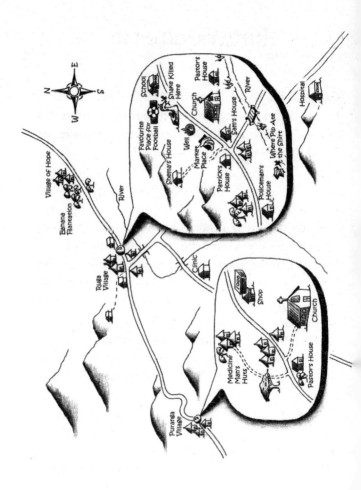

N
E W
S

Village of Hope

Banana Plantation

River

Ruga Village

Clinic

School

Snake Killed Here

Church

Pastor's House

River

Favourite Place for Football

Well

Sam's House

Where Pip Axe the Shirt

Hospital

Shena's House

Market Place

Patrick's House

Policeman's House

Shop

Church

Medicine Man's Huts

Pastor's House

Puranga Village

ONE

The Goatherd

Shema woke up and shivered. He clutched his well-worn blanket and wrapped it tighter around his thin little body. It couldn't be morning already, he thought, but looking through the little hole in the wall of his bedroom that made a window, he could see that the dawn was making the sky brighter, so he knew it must be so.

Shema lived in a small house that had a tin roof, but both the house and the roof had many holes in them. When it rained, they often got puddles on the floor. Like many traditional houses in Africa, the walls were built of bricks made from mud which had been dried in the sun, but now these were crumbling and there was no glass in the small squares cut into the walls for windows. Some houses in the village had wooden shutters, which could be put in place at night time, but Shema's house didn't have any, so it always seemed cold at night. In fact, it was a bit scary because, if you heard a noise, you thought perhaps somebody was climbing in!

"Shema," called his big sister, Ishimwe, "we need some water, please get up and go to the well."

"Coming!" Shema answered, but instead of getting up he snuggled down into his blanket for a few more minutes. He didn't want to get up!

"Shema!" his sister called again, this time in a louder voice. "Please, get the water for us!"

This time Shema sat up and folded his blanket, leaving it on his mattress. He didn't have a bed, or even a sheet, but shared a mattress made of foam with his small brother Maji. Maji was still fast asleep, but he was only five years old. Shema looked at him and smiled. He was such a funny little boy, always making his brother and sister laugh. Shema felt very grown up because now he was eight!

He rubbed his eyes and stretched. As he only had a few clothes and no night clothes, he just straightened his shorts and top. He had no shoes and his feet were always very dirty from walking on the mud floors in the house and on the dirt roads outside.

It was damp and chilly outside, so Shema found his sweater to put on over his rather old and dirty T-shirt. At least the rainy season was just about finished! He grabbed the yellow plastic jerrycan that he used to carry the water and began the walk down the valley to the well. It was a three kilometre walk, but he was used to that. Going down was easy; coming back up with a full can of water on your head was a different matter!

As he ran down the hill, Shema began to feel warmer. He could hear the birds singing in the blue-green eucalyptus trees and the sun was driving away the mist. There were lots of other people on the path, many of them also carrying the yellow cans to collect the water they needed for the day. Some were his friends.

"Hi Shema, how are you today?" called out his friend Sam.

"I'm fine," he called back. "How was your night?" (This is the usual morning greeting in Rwanda.)

"It was good," replied Sam. "But now I have to get the water before school."

"I wish I could go to school," sighed Shema. "I would love to learn to read and write! If I went to school perhaps I could one day be an airline pilot. Wouldn't it be wonderful to fly a plane and see other countries?"

"Wow, yes!" agreed Sam. Sometimes the boys saw planes in the sky and loved to watch them and wonder where they were going and who might be on them.

Shema had never been to school. Not only had his parents been killed in a terrible civil war, but all his relations apart from his sister and brother had also died, so now the three children lived together and looked after themselves. It was a hard life for them and they were very, very poor. Ishimwe was only twelve years old herself, but she tried hard to be a mother to the boys, growing and cooking food for them. Outside their house was a small plot of land where she grew millet, cassava, tomatoes and beans.

Ishimwe herself had gone to school for two years. Then the war came and most of the schools closed down. Children stayed at home with their parents, often hiding from the soldiers. So now, with no relatives to help them, she had to keep house, and as she was not able to read or write very well herself, she could not help her brothers to learn. She had no money to be able to send the boys to school, either, for although the classes in primary school were free, the students had to wear uniform and provide their own pencils and exercise books and that was too expensive.

Sam was also poor, but not as poor as Shema. He lived with his mum and grandparents, but his dad had also been killed in the war. He too had an older sister, called Grace, who was now at boarding school in the capital city of Kigali. Most of the senior schools were located in towns and the children went as boarders. So Sam only saw Grace in the long holiday, once a year. He missed having her around, for she used to help him with fetching the water and also explained his homework.

Sam, too, was eight years old and he and Shema had become best friends. They liked to play football together. They had made a ball by wrapping twine made from banana bark around lots of bits of old plastic bags. It had taken a long time to make and was their favourite toy.

"Where are you taking the goats today?" Sam asked his friend.

"I am going to the bushes around your school," Shema answered. "There are some good bushes there and while the goats are chewing I can sometimes hear the lessons you are learning, so I try to learn them, too."

Shema looked after some goats for a neighbour in their village and by doing this he earned a little money to help buy food. He liked the goats, giving them all names and talking to them through the day. The goats, too, were his friends.

"If you keep the goats there until after school, I'll meet you and we'll play football," suggested Sam.

By now they had reached the well and filled their cans with water. It was much harder returning home balancing the can on your head! Even though they did this journey every day, the boys always found lots to talk about as they walked along the track. Somehow, the water can did not seem so heavy when you had a friend to talk to as you walked!

When they reached the house where Sam lived, they saw his mother in the doorway waiting for them. Sam's house was a good one; the mud bricks had been coated with cement, which made it more waterproof. There were several rooms inside, but it was still not very big and was all on one floor, as were most of the village houses. Sam's mother always had a smile for Shema and a kind word to cheer him up. Today she called him over. "Can you spare a moment, Shema?"

"Yes Mama Grace," he answered. (A mother in Rwanda is always called after the name of her first child, that is why Shema called her Mama Grace.) "But I must not be long as Ishimwe is waiting for the water and I must collect the goats."

"I won't keep you long," Mama Grace assured him.

Shema went inside the house. The floor of this house had been cemented over and it felt cold to his bare feet. The sitting room had a sofa and two big chairs and Shema stroked them gently as he stood there. He didn't like to sit down in his dirty shorts in case he spoilt the cushion. The material felt so soft and special, so different from the hard bench in his house!

"Do you think that this will fit you and this fit Ishimwe?" asked Mama Grace as she held up two beautiful sweaters. They were lovely, not like the one he was wearing which had many holes in it. Shema just looked in amazement!

"These are for us?" he asked.

"Yes, if you would like them. I have been given them for my children, but they do not need them, so I thought you would like them." Shema's eyes were shining! He reached out and touched the sweaters. They were soft and warm.

"They are so wonderful, so wonderful, thank you, thank you so much!" he said. "I don't understand why you are so kind to me, I am not your child."

"Shema," Mama Grace said quietly, "You may not be my child but I love you and God loves you very much. When I talked to God he told me to give these to you."

Shema didn't really understand that. How could someone called God love him, just a poor uneducated goatherd, who was an orphan? He didn't know anything about God, but he did know that Sam's family went to the church in the village and talked a lot to this God and sang to him. They talked about "praying". It was all very strange to Shema and Ishimwe couldn't answer his questions about who God was either, because she didn't know. Perhaps he would learn about it at school one day, if he were ever able to go there. Anyway, he figured this God must be someone special if he told Mama Grace to give them these lovely sweaters!

Shema put his jerrycan of water back on his head and the precious bundle with the sweaters under his arm and almost ran with excitement back to the little house where he lived.

"Ishy, Ishy, come quickly, come quickly!" he yelled at the top of his voice, as he came near the door.

Ishimwe thought something terrible must have happened, so she came running to meet him, with Maji following just behind.

"Look, look! Sam's mother has given us a new sweater each," he explained as he put down the package and took the water container off his head. Shema then held up the lovely sweaters to show her. Suddenly he saw Maji's face and realised that there wasn't one for him. His happiness disappeared. What could he do? "I wonder," he thought to himself, "if I could I ask that God person for a sweater for a five year old? If he loves me like Mama Grace said he does, he would understand that Maji needs one, too."

TWO

School

Shema turned to his small brother as he gave Ishimwe her new sweater. "Maji," he said, "I am sorry there is not a sweater for you, but you can have this old one of mine, because it is very small and I am going to try to ask someone called Mister God to get you one. Sam's mother says he loves us, so I don't think he will mind if I ask him."

At this Maji began to smile. He was nearly always a cheerful little boy and he was pleased even to have Shema's old jumper. All three children dressed in their new sweaters and danced a little dance of joy for a few moments.

"Goodness, I shall be late for the goats!" cried Shema. So he took off his lovely sweater and folded it carefully, laying it on his mattress before running out of the house and down the path to collect the goats.

He went to Patrick's house and collected the twelve goats from the pen where they were kept. He also collected his big stick which he sometimes needed to swish the goats gently if they were going the wrong way and sometimes to beat down a thorn bush to clear the way. He knew one day he might need it to kill a snake, but, so far, thank goodness, he had not had to do that! Once or twice he had seen a small snake, but as he raised his stick it had quickly slithered away into the bushes. Shema knew that on the whole, most snakes were scared of humans and would not harm them unless they were cornered. But he also had heard many stories of people who had been bitten by snakes, so he wasn't going to take any chances!

The goats knew Shema very well and followed him as he led them up the red, dusty path to the school. They skipped and jumped, especially the baby kids. They were glad to be free after having been in the pen all night! Shema hardly needed to think about them as they darted around and chewed on the bushes along the path, so he began to think about asking God for a sweater. Could you only meet God at the church? Is that where he lived? Did it mean he had to go to the church with Mama Grace and Sam on Sunday? Today was only Tuesday and Sunday seemed a long time to wait. Shema thought that even if he did meet this God person on Sunday, it might take him a long time to get a sweater for Maji.

All this thinking had made Shema hungry and he was very glad that he had brought a banana with him. He sat on a rock and peeled it, then ate it slowly, making it last as long as possible, because it would be a long time before he was home again for his next meal.

Shema hummed a little song to himself as he watched the goats. When they had munched for a while, he took them further along the path and little by little they reached his favourite place; a large rock just outside the school, where he sat down.

The school was made up of four mud-brick buildings built in a square, each with three wooden doors, one for each classroom. Inside there were benches for the pupils, all facing the blackboard at the front. Each classroom had two windows, without glass, but outside were wooden shutters which could be closed when school was finished. It was a hot day so all the doors were open and Shema could hear the children being taught. Today the "baby" class was doing arithmetic. As the teacher asked them to add or take away different numbers, Shema tried to do the sums in his head, too. Sometimes he made marks with his stick on the sandy ground, if the sums were more difficult. Mostly the teacher spoke to the children in Kinyarwandan, which was his own language and that meant he was able to understand, but when they were learning French he didn't understand anything at all! Sitting there made him feel happy, though, as if he was really at school and it helped the time to pass quickly. He could see the goats easily as the area was very flat and there were very few trees.

At the end of the afternoon, the children finished their classes and came streaming out of the school. Some of them waved to him, for they were used to seeing him sitting on the rock watching the goats. He waved back, calling out a greeting.

Once school was finished, he knew it would not be long before Sam came to play. Sam often helped his teacher tidy up the classroom, making him one of the last children to leave. While he was waiting, Shema watched the teachers lock the classrooms, put big padlocks on the doors and close the shutters. One of them also waved to him and called out a greeting. He had noticed that the same little goatherd was often sitting near the school. "How are you?" called the teacher.

"I'm fine," Shema replied. The teacher walked over towards him and for a moment Shema was afraid that he might tell him off for sitting so near the school.

"You like to come here and graze your goats," the teacher remarked with a smile. "I often see you here."

"Yes, sir," Shema replied with relief, seeing the teacher was friendly. "I like to hear the children learning."

"Would you like to come to school?"

"Oh yes, sir, so very much, but I am an orphan and have to look after the goats. There is no money for me to come to school."

"What is your name, son?" asked the teacher.

"My name is Kabisa Shema," Shema replied, giving his full name. In Rwanda, people say their surname first, then the name they are usually called by.

"Well, young man, God loves you and I will pray that he will make a way for you to come to school."

"Thank you, sir," said Shema, as the teacher walked away. He thought how strange it was that two people had told him today that this person called

God loved him. As he was wondering about it, he saw Sam running towards him, kicking the ball as he ran. Sam also had a bottle with some water and they had a drink before they started to play. They found some sticks to mark a goal post and had great fun playing football together. Every now and then Shema paused to make sure all the goats were fine. They had been playing for quite a while, when he noticed that one of the kids was missing. "Sam!" he exclaimed. "I must stop and look for little Pip, I can't see him!"

"I'll help you," offered Sam.

"You stay with the eleven here and I will go and hunt for Pip," replied Shema.

He took his stick, went down to the bushes and began to call, "Pip, Pip!" But Pip didn't come straight away like he usually did. Shema began to get worried. Pip was quite young and didn't usually go far from his mother's side. Then he heard a bleating noise, and sure enough, there was Pip, behind some bushes, looking quite sad and lost.

"Come here, you rascal," said Shema, not really cross with the goat, but very relieved to see him safe and well. Pip looked happy to hear Shema's voice and followed him back to the rest of the flock.

The boys decided it was time to go home, so they began the journey back. Sam began to tell Shema that he had heard a story about a sheep that was lost and how a very good shepherd had left the ninety nine other sheep in the fold and gone out at night searching for the lost one.

"Did he find it?" asked Shema.

"Yes," replied Sam, "and there was a big party because the lost sheep had been found. It is a story from the Bible. Mama says the Good Shepherd is Jesus, God's Son, and he is looking for us to belong to him."

"It's a good story," said his friend. "I am glad that the lost sheep got found. I would hate Pip to be lost all night." He paused for a little while, not wanting to look stupid, but then he plucked up courage and asked his friend, "If I came with you on Sunday, would Mister God let me ask him something?" Sam looked puzzled.

"Well . . . it's not quite like that, you can't actually see God." Shema looked disappointed. "I can't explain it very well," continued Sam, "but I am sure Mama will talk to you and I would like you to come with me to church. I would like it very much."

"Then I will ask Ishimwe if I can come, but I do have to ask this God person something very important."

"Race you home!" said Sam and began to run, with Shema just behind him and twelve goats all around them. They arrived hot and tired at Patrick's house. Sam helped his friend put the goats in the pen before he went home.

Ishimwe had cooked some beans and some rice and Shema was really hungry. It had been a long day and he had so many things to think about. He told his brother and sister about the teacher who had talked to him and about Pip who had run off and got lost. Then the children lit a candle and went outside to wash with what was left of the cold water in the jerrycan. It had been an exciting day for Shema. As he went to bed he stroked the new sweater and whispered, "Mister God, I don't know who you are, but I would like to meet you and tell you about my sweater, and ask you for another one, if that isn't too cheeky, for my little brother Maji. He's only five. And, Mister God, there is something else, too, I really, really want to go to school! I heard today that you have a boy called Jesus who looks after sheep like I look after goats. That was a good story about him finding the lost sheep like I found Pip."

Shema had just been mumbling under his breath; he had no idea that he had been praying and that God had heard his prayer.

THREE

The Sunday Miracle

The days went by quickly and very soon it was Sunday. Shema told Ishimwe, after he had collected the water, that he wanted to go to the church in the village that day.

"But what about the goats?" asked Ishimwe. "They need to be looked after every day, or you won't get paid and someone else will get your job."

"I hadn't thought about that," said Shema, sadly. "Of course I can't go."

In every country of the world, animals need looking after every day. Farmers and goatherds do not get weekends off. Even in other jobs, many people in Rwanda have to work every day to get enough money to buy their food.

Shema felt really fed up. Sometimes it would be so nice to do what you wanted, instead of having to look after the stupid goats every day! He kicked a stone with his bare foot, feeling very cross as he went to collect the animals.

He stomped to Patrick's house, undid the goat pen and drove the goats out. They weren't used to him being grumpy and skipped out very quickly. With his big stick he swished their backsides, not too hard, but enough to show he was in a bad mood. Life wasn't fair! Why couldn't he go to school or church or just out to play whenever he wanted?

Shema drove the goats a long way, close to the river. Now the hot, dry season had returned, there was only a trickle of water in the river, but the goats still liked drinking there. At the stream some people were washing their clothes, even though the water was brown and muddy. Only very rich people had a tap in their house and the water carried from the well was so precious that the river seemed a good place for washing clothes and then they could be put on the bushes to dry in the sun.

Suddenly Shema felt better as he thought of his sister who also worked so hard, doing the washing, cooking and gardening for them all. It wasn't fair for her either. He gave a big sigh. If only they still had their mum and dad, how different everything would be! He felt a tear falling down his face, but quickly wiped it away. It was not good for a big boy of eight to cry!

Once the goats had drunk from the stream, Shema tied them up to the bushes with string made from banana bark. He gave them as much string as he could so that they could walk around the bush and nibble the branches. He knew then that even Pip could not run away and get lost. Then he took off his clothes and ran down to the water himself and began to splash around. Soon some other children began to join him and they laughed as they splashed each other! Shema was very tempted to drink the water, but he knew he might get sick if he did. He was thirsty though and hungry. It was a long time to go all day without food or drink. After a while the mothers were calling the other children, so Shema got out of the water too and went to dress. To his dismay, he couldn't find his T-shirt! He put his trousers on and looked everywhere. Then he saw it! Pip, the kid, had found it and was eating it! Shema couldn't help it, the tears really came now! They just poured down his cheeks. Even though Pip looked so funny with half a T-shirt hanging out of his mouth, Shema couldn't laugh, he just howled! His sobs were so loud that a crowd of people soon gathered around him.

"Whatever has happened?" asked one lady. "Has a snake bitten you or eaten one of your goats?"

"No," sobbed Shema, "it's the goat who has eaten my shirt!" The people around started to giggle as they saw Pip with a bit of shirt left in his mouth, but the more they laughed, the louder Shema's sobs became.

"You don't understand," he cried, "it is the only one I have and my sister can't afford to get another one." One of the women stopped laughing.

"I'm sorry," she said. "It is just that the goat looked so funny. Don't cry so much. If you don't mind a shirt that is still a bit wet, you can have one from my washing. It is quite old, but I think it will fit you. It is too tight for my son. I think I know who you are, one of the family of orphans who live on the hill over there?" She pointed towards the area where the three children lived. Shema nodded.

"Yes, I do live there, with my sister and brother." The woman went to the bushes where she had spread her washing to dry. She picked up a T-shirt and was bringing it to Shema when she suddenly turned and went back to her laundry. Shema thought she had changed her mind and sighed deeply. But she turned around again, picked something else up and came back to him.

"Try this on," she said, handing him a smart green T-shirt. "And if I remember your family properly, you have a small brother, don't you? Take this home for him. I told my husband only this morning we would have to buy a bigger one for our youngest son." In her hand she held a bright blue sweater! It looked just the right size for Maji! It was a miracle! Mister God must have known about Maji after all, or perhaps Sam had somehow managed to have a word with him!

Even though it was still a bit damp, Shema pulled the T-shirt over his head. It fitted him well! He decided to keep it on, it would soon finish drying in the sunshine! A big smile spread across his face. Shema said a great big "thank you" to the kind woman who had given the clothes to him.

He forgot how thirsty he had been, he was now so excited that he just wanted to go home and see Maji's face when he gave him the sweater! He went over to naughty Pip and instead of swishing him with his stick, he rubbed his neck and kissed his nose! He no longer felt fed up about not being able to go to church, he felt very happy and began to sing to the goats! He sang them a song which the children sang in the school, which he had learnt as he listened to them:

"*Imana ni nzaa, Imana ni nzaa, Imana ni nzaa, Ni nzaa cyane!*"

"God is so good, God is so good, God is so good, He's so good to me!"

At the end of the afternoon, Shema untied the goats, and they began their journey home. He had tied Maji's sweater around his waist, over his new T-shirt. The shirt was much nicer than the one the goat had eaten, it wasn't full of holes like that had been! It soon finished drying on his body and felt very comfortable.

As he ran into his home, he could smell the rice cooking. Mm, it smelt good! He was so hungry!

"Maji, Maji!" Shema called to his little brother, who was watching his sister cook. "Look, I don't know how, but Mister God must have known about you needing a sweater, because I have one for you!" Maji looked at the blue sweater and began to jump up and down with delight. But Ishimwe looked puzzled and was frowning.

"Shema," she said, "you must tell me the truth. You haven't been stealing, have you? You have another shirt on, a nice clean one without holes and now you have a sweater for Maji. Where did they come from?

I am very worried. No matter how poor we are, I will not have you stealing. We might all end up in prison!"

"Ishy," replied Shema, "you know I would not steal. I know I am sometimes disobedient but truly, I would not steal. These things have been given to me and somehow I know it is to do with this Mister God who people keep saying loves us. Sit down and I will tell you both the whole story."

They all sat on their little bench with their rice and beans and Shema told them all about his day, how fed up he had felt and how the goat had eaten his shirt. They all ended up laughing as they listened to this part of the story, for Rwandans love to hear stories. It was a happy little family that went to bed that night. Shema pulled his blanket over him and looked at the face of his small brother. He looked so happy and had gone to sleep clutching his new sweater. Shema whispered quietly to himself, "Well, I don't know, but Mister God must have laughed too at Pip eating my T-shirt, because he had something better for me! Wherever you are, Mister God, thank you!"

The Rwandans have a saying, that by day God goes all around the world, but he comes home to Rwanda to sleep at night! Shema had never thought about the saying before, but he decided it must be true!

FOUR

Maji Becomes Sick

Several weeks had passed since the day when the goat had eaten the T-shirt. The weather began to change once again. The long, hot, dry days were over and now the rains had started. In one way, everyone was pleased, especially Ishimwe, who had seeds to plant in the little garden. It meant there was more water available, the dried-up bushes and grass began to get green and the crops would grow. These were good things, but other things were not so nice. Shema often got wet and cold as he went to fetch the water. He was so glad of his new sweater! When he took the goats out, the paths were now slippery and the cold, red mud squished between his toes. He would look for a tree so that he could shelter underneath it while he watched the goats, and he had a polythene bag, which he had made into a hat, to cover his head. He wasn't able to go near the school so often, as there was no tree nearby to shelter under, neither was he able to play football so often with Sam. He kept trying to be cheerful, because he knew that the rain meant that they would have food next year. But in the night, the noise of the rain kept him awake as it pounded on the tin roof and often it trickled through the holes in the roof and down the mud walls onto the floor, making it muddy and slippery, even indoors. His blanket was too thin, as well. He and Maji cuddled together to try to keep warm and get more sleep.

One night Shema noticed that Maji was getting hotter and hotter, then he started to shiver and shake. He seemed really ill. Shema called his sister to come and they tried to wake Maji up, but couldn't.

"I think he must have malaria!" cried Ishimwe in alarm. "What are we going to do?" (Malaria is a disease carried by mosquitoes. Many people in Africa become sick and even die from this illness.)

"He is so hot, we ought to bathe him in cold water," suggested Shema. His sister thought this was a good idea, so they lit a candle and went out to find some water. There was enough left from the day's supply to put into a basin and with an old rag, Ishimwe gently bathed her little brother.

The children didn't know what else to do, so took it in turns to keep awake and bathe Maji through the night. When morning came, he was still very ill. Ishimwe untied her rag where she kept the few coins they earned from minding the goats and other small jobs she was sometimes able to do. There was very little money. She carefully counted it to see if there was enough to go to the clinic and buy medicine. Ishimwe was so worried about Maji, she decided she would try. She told Shema to stay as near to their house as he could while he was minding the goats, for she would have to leave Maji in the house while she walked to the clinic and back, which would take several hours.

Shema ran as fast as he could down to Patrick's house to collect the goats and took them as near to his own house as he dared. If they went too near the house he knew they would eat everything in Ishimwe's garden, but he wanted to stay close to little Maji, too. Once again, he found himself talking. "Mister God person, wherever you are, can you help us? We don't want Maji to die!" It sounded silly, talking to someone you could not see, but, after all, he had helped with the sweater, so it was worth a try!

Every now and then Shema ran back to the house and bathed Maji with cold water. His little brother was so hot! He didn't recognise Shema and was talking nonsense all the time. Indeed, he was very ill.

The hours went by and Shema longed for Ishimwe to return. He was so glad when he heard her running up the path to the house. She had a few tablets folded in a piece of paper. It was all their money could buy. She crushed one of the tablets until it was a powder, mixed it with a little water just as the nurse had told her, then tried to spoon it into Maji's mouth. It was really difficult to get him to swallow it, but she tried and little by little Maji took the medicine.

Now that his sister was back home, Shema could take the goats back to their owner. Patrick was waiting for them. "You are late!" he said. "It's almost dark!"

"Oh Patrick, I'm sorry, I couldn't come before,

because I was waiting for my sister to come home."
He then told him the whole story of Maji's illness.
Patrick helped him put the goats in the pen, then
looked at the young lad.

"Shema," he said, "you could go to a medicine
man. Their magic is very strong."

"But we have spent all our money on tablets,"
replied Shema. "Ishimwe says we can only wait and
see if they work."

"Over two hills and in a village called Puranga
lives a cousin of mine," replied Patrick. "He works
strong magic. Go to him and say I sent you. I will find
someone to take care of the goats while you go."

Shema looked at Patrick and thought about what
he had said. He didn't really know much about
medicine men, except that they made magic spells
and strange medicines and everyone was frightened
of them. In the old days, before there were clinics,
everyone went to the traditional medicine men, or
witch doctors as they were sometimes called, but
Shema knew that now most people would rather go
to a doctor or nurse to get help. Still, when that failed
people sometimes did try the old magic spells. Shema
shivered with fear when he thought about it. Deep
inside he didn't want to leave the village or visit a
medicine man, but if Maji was dying, what else could
he do?

At home that night Shema told Ishimwe what
Patrick had told him about his cousin. Neither of the
children was very happy about his suggestion and

they decided to wait until the morning to see if Maji
was any better. When they went to bed, Maji was still
shivering and shaking and talking rubbish to himself.
His older brother and sister were very scared.

Even though Shema was tired, he could not sleep
well that night. Several times he bathed Maji with
cold water when he seemed too hot, then sometimes
Maji was shivering, so he covered him with his own
blanket and then felt cold himself. Shema was glad
when the morning light began to shine though the
window. He got up, splashed some cold water over
his face, grabbed the yellow jerrycan and ran as fast
as he could to the well. He was already on his way
home when he met Sam on his way to fetch water. He
was in such a hurry that he just quickly told Sam the
news of Maji's sickness, then ran on home.

Maji was no better, so even though he was very
scared, Shema decided he had to go to the medicine
man. It would be a very long walk and he didn't
know if he could get there and home in one day, so
took his stick; somehow it made him feel stronger
and safer. Ishimwe gave him two little sweet bananas
and some boiled water in a plastic bottle. "Be very,
very careful," she said, as he set off. "Try to be back
before dark." Nobody liked to be out in the dark.
Shema had no torch to show him the path and he
might meet a monkey or a hyena!

FIVE

Journey to the Medicine Man

The first part of the journey was not too bad. The sun was still not too hot and Shema knew the way over the first hill. Then, as the day wore on, Shema's legs became heavy and tired. He found a rock to sit on and ate a banana and had just a little drink. He had no idea how long the journey would take and did not want to run out of water. The sky was looking very dark and Shema knew it was going to rain. He got up and began to run along the path, but when a storm began, the thunder and lightening made him feel scared, and the huge raindrops quickly soaked his clothes. As he ran along the path his feet splashed in the puddles and the red mud became thicker and thicker, making it very hard to walk. Shema could feel his heart beating loudly in his chest and he tried not to cry. "I'll get there, I'll get there," he said to himself. "I have to get help for Maji! Maji must not die."

Finally, Shema made it over the top of the second hill and could see Puranga village below. That gave him the courage to continue. It was almost dark when he reached the village. He was very hungry by now and his second banana was looking brown and squashed, so he decided he had to eat it. He washed it down with a small drink from the precious water bottle and walked boldly into the main street.

When he saw a little shop, Shema mustered up all his courage and asked the shopkeeper where the medicine man lived. The shopkeeper looked at the bedraggled little boy and frowned. "What do you want with him?" he asked.

"He has strong magic and my neighbour, who is his cousin, has sent me to him, so that my little brother can be made well," replied Shema.

"Well, young man, be very careful," warned the shopkeeper. As he said this, Shema felt really frightened, just as he had when Patrick had first told him about the medicine man. In fact, Shema felt so scared that he just wanted to run all the way back home, even though it was getting dark, but thinking of how ill Maji was made him stay.

"I will be careful, I only want medicine," he said.

"All right, go to the big thorn tree past the last house you can see from here. Then at the thorn tree is a small path that leads to three old, round, mud houses with grass roofs. There you will find the medicine man. But be very careful and do not say that I did not warn you. You are a very young boy to visit him on your own."

Feeling even more scared than ever, Shema walked on. He could feel the eyes of the shopkeeper watching him as he made his way to the thorn tree. He felt too scared to go quickly, but tried to walk as if he felt confident. What did the shopkeeper mean about being very careful and warning him? Surely it would be all right, he was only asking for medicine. Why was everyone so scared of the medicine man? Was it because he had magic powers to cast spells for bad as well as good? All sorts of thoughts were going round Shema's head. Usually he liked adventures, but this one didn't seem any fun at all. Perhaps that was because Maji was so ill and he had to make a journey so far from his home. He wished his friend Sam was with him. He wanted somebody to talk to.

At the thorn tree Shema could just see the three round houses. They were very old traditional huts with thatched grass roofs, not iron sheets like most houses. It was quite dark by now, but he could see a small light in one of them. Slowly he made his way towards them.

"Hello!" he tried to shout when he reached the house with the light, but his voice was almost gone and his throat was very dry because he was so frightened. A very tall man came out.

"Who are you and what do you want at this time of day?" he asked Shema in a very gruff voice.

"Please, sir, I am Kabisa Shema and your cousin Patrick who lives in the village of Ruga, two hills away, has sent me to find you. I have a very sick little brother and he says you have strong magic medicine that can cure him. He told me to come even though I have no money. Please help me!" Poor Shema was shaking by now with fear, hunger and tiredness. It had been such a long and difficult journey. His clothes were wet and muddy and he longed to be back home.

The man looked him up and down. Shema felt as if he was looking right inside him. His instinct was to turn round and run away as fast as he could. There was something about this place that seemed bad. It also had a horrible smell of rotting meat that made his stomach feel as if he was going to be sick.

"Oh yes, I can help," said the man. Shema looked relieved. "But as you have no money you will have to do what I want you to do, to pay for the magic," he added.

"I see," answered Shema, but in fact he did not see at all and just stood rooted to the ground, not knowing what else to do or say.

"You had better come in then," the man said, as he reached out and grabbed poor Shema very roughly, pulling him into the dark hut.

"Lie down over there for the night." He pointed to a dirty blanket on the floor. "We will do magic tomorrow." The medicine man smiled at Shema, but it was not a kind smile like Mama Grace's smile, it was a queer sort of smile that made him uneasy. But by now Shema was too scared to do anything except obey the medicine man and lie on the blanket. Eventually, from sheer exhaustion, hungry as he was, he dropped off to sleep.

SIX

Help Is on the Way

Sam had fetched his water as usual and taken it home. Mama Grace was waiting for him with his exercise book and a packed lunch for school wrapped in a banana leaf. "No Shema with you today?" she had asked. "You haven't fallen out, have you?"

"No, Mum," he answered. "Shema was very early getting water today, because Maji is sick. He was nearly home when I met him. He said he had to go on a journey to get medicine."

"I expect he is going to the clinic," said Mama Grace, as she hugged her son and sent him on his way.

Throughout the morning Mama Grace found herself thinking about the three children in the house alone and wondered how they managed. Shema always seemed so cheerful, but he did look thin. Now Maji was sick! He was so small. Mama Grace felt sorry for the children, and decided she must visit them to see if she could do something to help. In church the pastor had preached only last Sunday about helping widows and orphans. She was a widow herself, but these children had no mother or father to care for them. She called out to her own mother, the Old Lady.

38

"Are you all right this morning, Mama, if I go to visit the orphans on the hill? You know the ones, Sam's friend Shema and his brother and sister. I hear the small boy is sick."

"Of course," croaked the Old Lady, who now had almost no voice and could only walk a little, using a stick that Sam had made for her from a branch of a tree. "You go and take a few francs from me." She held out a dirty, crumpled bank note that she had taken from her pocket.

"That is kind of you, thank you, Mama," said her daughter and she added some money of her own to give to Ishimwe. Next she went to her kitchen, which was a little shack behind the house and put some milk, fresh that morning from her own prized cow, into a bottle, to take for the sick boy. Her father, the Old Man, was sitting outside in the yard. He smiled at his daughter.

"Don't you worry about anything, my girl," he said. "I may be old but I can still take care of things here!" After the war, Mama Grace's parents had come to live with her. Everyone knew and loved them and called them "Old Man and Old Lady" or "The Old People". It was really a title of respect, for all older people are respected in Rwanda. They are even called "The Library" sometimes, for who else do you go to when you want to know something and don't have any books? They have all the wisdom and knowledge because they have lived so many years!

It took Mama Grace a few minutes to walk up the

hill to the children's home. She was sad as she looked at the house, it was almost falling down! She thought to herself that she must ask her pastor if there was any way the church could help these orphans. Nobody in the church was rich, but these children were only just able to survive.

As she reached the door, Sam's mother called out a greeting to Ishimwe and asked to come in. Ishimwe was surprised to see Mama Grace, but warmly invited her to come in. The older lady gave the young girl a hug, which made tears spring to Ishimwe's eyes. It reminded her of when her mother was alive and hugged her! Mama Grace asked to see Maji and found tears in her own eyes when she looked at the little boy lying on his old mattress, so very ill and with such a fever.

"I have brought some milk for Maji and a few francs from the Old Lady and me," said Mama Grace as she held out her gifts to Ishimwe. Again, tears came to the young girl's eyes and she swallowed hard to try and say "thank you" without crying.

Mama Grace then asked about medicine and would Shema be back soon from the clinic?

Ishimwe told her that they had bought all the medicine they could afford yesterday, but now Shema had gone along to the medicine man to beg for strong medicine to save Maji's life.

When she heard this, Mama Grace felt a chill go down her spine. Shema could be in danger! Medicine men had a reputation for being bad people and often making evil spells. Sometimes they took people's money but the magic spells made the sick person worse and not better. She knew, too, that as Shema had no money, the medicine man might not let him go home, but keep him as a servant or even make him an apprentice medicine man! She asked where he lived and what time Shema had left to walk there. Ishimwe told her all she knew about Patrick's cousin.

As she sat and listened, Sam's mother knew she had to do something to help. But what could she do? Mama Grace was a Christian and so, as she sat on the hard wooden bench, she quietly started to pray about these things to God, her heavenly Father. She needed him not only to help find Shema quickly and bring him safely home, but also to heal Maji, who was indeed a very ill child. She knew, only too well, how many children died in her country from illnesses like malaria, because of lack of treatment. She needed to share her own fears and worries about the situation with God and know that he would help her. She also asked God what she should do about it all. After a few moments, Mama Grace turned to Ishimwe.

"Ishimwe," she said, "I can see that Maji is very sick. It is bad for him to be in this house where the rain is coming in. He is too weak to walk and I cannot carry him all the way to my house. I am going to get some help and I will get him carried to the hospital. We will worry about the money to pay the bills later, but for now, we must get him medical help. When he is in the hospital you must stay and look after him and I will go and find Shema and bring him back to my house. Don't worry any more, God will help us."

After giving Ishimwe another hug, Mama Grace began to run down the slippery mud track back to the village. Her heart was pounding so loudly she thought everyone in the village must be able to hear it! She was very worried, both for Maji, whether they would get him to the hospital in time to save his life, but also for Shema, for she knew his life was in danger too, in the house of the medicine man. If this man found out that Shema was an orphan with no parents to protect him, he could well take advantage of him. She dreaded the thought that dear Shema might be held captive and taught how to make evil spells!

First of all, Mama Grace went back to her own house to check on her elderly parents. She told them all the troubles of the three orphans and that she needed to find some men who would carry Maji to the hospital, then she would have to somehow go and find Shema who was also in danger. Her parents said they would be fine and would look after Sam when he came home, if she was still away. Mama Grace gave a big sigh of relief and silently thanked God for her mother and father, then asked him to help her rescue the boys.

It was raining again, so Mama Grace wrapped her *kitenge* cloth, which is a large brightly coloured cloth with many uses, around her shoulders and head, and tried to avoid the big puddles as she ran to the nearby little shops. There were always people sitting around inside the shops, or outside if the sun was shining. She ran into the nearest shop and to her delight, she recognised some of her friends from the church, sitting and chatting.

"Come and join us, Mama Grace," invited one of them, "you look really out of breath. Have you been running?"

"I have a big problem to solve and need help very quickly," she replied as she tried to get her breath back.

"Then tell us about it and we will all consider it together!" her friend answered.

So Mama Grace sat down and began to sip the hot, sweet, milky tea that had been handed to her. Indeed, she needed this mug of "*chai*" to calm her as she began to tell them the story of Maji, Ishimwe and Shema. Instantly four of the men who were in the shop got up and said they would carry Maji to the hospital. Mama Grace looked relieved, as it was a very long way to the hospital and the men were both kind and strong. They went to fetch the "ambulance", which was not really an ambulance at all, but a woven stretcher looking like a huge basket, carried on poles which rested on the men's shoulders. Out in the country, where there are no vehicles like our ambulances to race patients to the hospital, a big stretcher is the best way to carry a sick person to get help. The men began to run up the hill towards the children's house. Mama Grace gave a big sigh and whispered "thank you" to God, for she knew she had done all she could to save Maji. Now it was Shema's turn. This was a much bigger problem and although she was a grown lady, she still felt scared.

SEVEN

The Evil Hut

Shema woke with a start before dawn. Where was he? What was the horrible smell in the house? It was still dark and he tried to get up, but his legs were aching from the long walk in the rain. Gradually Shema remembered where he was and why he had come to this horrible place. Why had Patrick sent him here? He had thought Patrick was a friend, a good man. Perhaps he didn't know that his cousin lived in a dirty, smelly hut that made him shiver with fear. Shema had hoped that he would just have been given some medicine and been able to go straight home. Now it seemed that he would have to stay and work to pay for the medicine. If he didn't get it soon, then it might be too late to help Maji! The thought of that made Shema want to cry, but he knew he had to be brave.

What could he do? He wanted to try to escape and run home but as he tried to call out "help!" his voice just seemed to dry up inside his mouth. He knew, too, that these huts were away from the road and the other houses, so nobody would hear him anyway.

This time, when the tears came, he could not even wipe them away. They fell down his face and felt salty on his lips. He realised he was also very thirsty. From somewhere deep inside him Shema felt he should talk to Mister God, even though he had never met him and didn't know where he was.

"Mister God," whispered Shema through his dry mouth, "you gave us warm clothes and Mama Grace and the teacher both said you loved us. I don't know how you can, but help me now, please help me!" Shema heard a cockerel crow and knew it must be nearly dawn. He lay quietly, wondering what would happen next. If he tried to escape, he wouldn't be able to get any medicine for Maji, but he wanted so much to run away. As he thought of Maji he wondered if he was any better and he also wondered who would get water for Ishimwe. He so wanted to be back in his own home! He decided that he would never grumble about having to fetch water ever again!

As it grew lighter he could see more of the room. It was dirty and smelly and every now and then he saw a mouse or a rat. The noise of the rats frightened him. Suddenly, he heard footsteps and his body began to shake with fear. The medicine man came in and stood over him.

"You are awake then," he said roughly to the boy.

"Yes, sir. Please can I have the medicine now to take back to my little brother?"

"All in good time, boy. First we have to prepare the medicine." Poor little Shema trembled with fear, almost being sick as the man bent over him and handed him a plastic cup with some water. The little boy drank it, gulping it down with big gulps.

He was so thirsty! He had some cold *posho* placed
into his hand, not even on a plate. *Posho* is thick
maize porridge which isn't always very nice even
when it is hot. It was so revolting that Shema could
hardly swallow a mouthful, but he knew he had to
eat something. It was like eating cold glue! Shema
longed for the safety of his own house, with the
boiled water that Ishimwe gave him to drink and her
nice food to eat. Would he ever see his family again?
They seemed so far away!

After his horrible breakfast, the man told Shema to
sit on the ground in the corner of the room until it
was time to prepare the medicine. Then the medicine
man went outside and closed the door.

Soon Shema heard another man's voice outside
the hut. The medicine man apparently had another
customer. Shema heard the man asking for help
because he could not get work and his family were
starving. The medicine man told him that he needed
to bring two chickens. They would be killed and
the magic performed. It seemed the medicine man
was now busy and he had no time to make medicine
for Shema. He began to chant, which sounded
queer and nasty. With a jolt, Shema realised that
this man was a bad man and he wondered how evil
magic could do a good thing like make Maji well.
When the medicine man looked at Shema, it was
not with a kind face or any concern for him or his
sick brother, there was just a hard, strange smile.
Shema knew inside himself that the man made only

evil magic and bad spells. He also was afraid of what the medicine man might make him do to pay for the medicine for Maji. He felt sure it would be something bad. But now, knowing the one thing he could do, Shema whispered another prayer. "Mister God, please rescue me." He didn't really understand what praying was, but he knew Sam talked to this "God person" and that God was good. That made him think of the song he had learnt when he was minding the goats near the school:

"God is so good, God is so good, God is so good, He's so good to me!"

Shema began to sing it to himself in his head, then gradually he became bolder and began to sing it with his voice, although very softly. Somehow it helped him. He didn't feel quite so shaky and scared. It was almost as if a good power had come into the room. At least, it did not seem so evil any more.

Shema had no idea of the time. The hut was quite dark and he couldn't see the sun that always helped him to know the time of day. It seemed as if hours had passed, and he began to drift off to sleep, but this time it was a peaceful sleep.

Mama Grace had no idea how she could reach and save Shema, but as she began the long walk over the hills, she too was talking to God. "My Father," she prayed, "Please help me, and protect me from evil on this journey. May I be in time to save Shema from any harm the medicine man might plan. If he is planning to kidnap him and make him a servant, help me to rescue him."

Mama Grace was not so young as Shema and had to rest more often on the way. When at last she reached Puranga Village, the daylight had almost gone and she was very tired. She knew she was walking slowly now, but she just had no more strength. Stopping to rest for a moment, Mama Grace became aware of singing. It was a hymn; there must be a church nearby! Sure enough, in the distance she could see lights and the singing was definitely coming from that place. So she struggled on a little further to the church.

When she arrived, Mama Grace almost fell over the porch, she was so exhausted! A lady came to help her and drew her into the building. A group of women were sitting on benches having a meeting, but they stopped singing when they saw Mama Grace. Gently, the lady who had helped her in sat her down and asked her who she was and why she had come.

When she had got her breath back, Mama Grace told the group of women the reason for her visit. They looked at each other in horror, then one of them spoke. "We know that man. He is a very bad medicine man. He may plan to hurt the boy, or make him his servant. He is evil and cruel. We never go near his huts." Another lady spoke up.

"We are here praying," she said firmly. "We have been praying and praising God because he is all-powerful, so we will pray now that he will help you and protect you and deliver this child." They all started to pray, everyone at the same time. The praying made Mama Grace feel strong again, because her strength came from God and his great power!

"I must get to Shema straight away!" she said, when they had stopped praying. An old lady looked up.

"Now, my dear," she said to Mama Grace. "The daylight is gone. You can do nothing until morning. Come with me and eat and rest. My husband is the pastor here and I am sure he will go with you tomorrow, as soon as it is light. We must trust God to protect this child for tonight." Mama Grace knew that the old lady was talking sense. She went with her to her house and was looked after so kindly. How she thanked God for her lovely meal and a clean mattress and blanket for sleeping! The pastor, when he had heard the story, had prayed too for the three orphans and had promised to go with Mama Grace to the medicine man as soon as it was light.

Exhausted, Mama Grace lay down to sleep, knowing that her heavenly Father had led her safely to this place and to these kind folk who would help her. It was a miracle! She trusted that she would be in time to save Shema from being hurt or forced to become a servant. She had a sense of peace and felt that God was all powerful and all loving.

Just as he had promised, the elderly pastor and his wife woke Mama Grace as soon as it was light. There was hot, sweet tea to drink and maize porridge to eat, which warmed Mama Grace and made her feel stronger. Together they prayed before starting on the journey to the medicine man's huts.

The old pastor prayed, "Dear Lord, our God, we know this man is very evil and probably intends to harm this little boy. Thank you that you are more powerful than any magic, and that your love can destroy evil. We are trusting you to help us now, please cover us with your protection. We ask in Jesus' name, Amen."

Then, not knowing what they would find or what they would do, he and Mama Grace set out.

EIGHT

The Rescue

It had been a long day for Shema. He had sat in the corner of the dark room for most of the time, while the medicine man was chanting in a horrid voice and making spells and killing the chickens for the man who had come to ask for help to find a job. It was horrible to listen to. From time to time Shema drifted off to sleep, but when he was awake he sang the song "God is so good" to himself. It really helped him to feel less frightened and kept his spirits up. Later in the day, the medicine man had come in for a short while, giving Shema a few scraps of food and a drink of some dirty water from a tin mug. All the time the man kept very close to him, not giving him any chance to run away. Shema wondered what was to happen and if the medicine man would make a spell for Maji, but he was too frightened to ask. He wondered if Maji was still alive and if Ishimwe was now worried about him, as it had been so long since he set off on this journey. It seemed to Shema that it was years ago that he had been safe in his own house with his brother and sister. He wished he hadn't listened to Patrick and taken his advice and that he had never come to this horrible place.

When it began to get dark, the medicine man came

back into the hut and talked to Shema. "I have been very busy today," he said. "The man who needed me was able to pay me. You cannot have spells or strong magic unless you pay well. You will have to pay for your brother's magic. You will pay by serving me. When I need water, you will fetch it, or if I need food, you will cook it. You will clean up for me and do all I tell you. Don't even think about running away to your home because I will make sure that Patrick brings you back to me." Then he began to laugh in such a way that it made Shema's body shake with fear. It was the sort of laugh that had no music in it, but rather, made shivers go down your spine!

In spite of his terror, Shema found the song about God being good was in his mind and he began to sing it out loud. As he did, he found his shaking was stopping and his mouth was less dry. The song, however, made the medicine man mad! He started to shout and rave and yell at Shema, telling him to shut up! He pushed him back into the corner of the room. "Wait until tomorrow when you start to work for me! You won't sing then!" he threatened.

But Shema sang himself to sleep. How glad he was that he had listened to the children in the school and learned the song with them! The song seemed to have a power in it. This God person must be very powerful, Shema thought to himself. Surely he was more powerful than this medicine man! "Please help me, Mister God," he said again to himself, as he drifted off to sleep. "Please get me away from this horrible place. And please," he added, "please make Maji well without me having to be this man's servant."

It was just getting light when he woke up. Shema saw the medicine man picking up his jerrycan and leaving the hut. Shema thought how odd it was that even this powerful man needed to have water collected. He obviously couldn't make magic that would produce water.

Shema sat up, glad to know the man had gone out. Then he heard the cock crowing and a rat scuttling over the grass roof. "What was disturbing it?" he wondered. Then he thought he heard another shuffling sort of noise and another, but he couldn't recognise what the noise might be. It seemed to go all around the hut. Was there a wild animal prowling around? He felt very scared by the noises.

"Shema, Shema, are you there?" he heard a friendly voice whisper. At first he thought he was dreaming.

"Shema!" came the voice again.

"I'm here, I'm here, inside this hut!" he tried to shout as loud as he could, but his mouth was dry. The door slowly opened and some light came into the room, along with two people! Shema felt big, strong arms lift him and he looked up into the face of a kind old man. Then in the semi-darkness, he saw another person. It was Mama Grace!

"Oh, Mama Grace!" he cried, "Mama Grace!" He couldn't say any more because the tears were pouring down his face.

"Let's go," said the kind old man. "We must get away from here at once. If the medicine man finds us, he may try to harm us all." Shema stopped crying and found his voice.

"He has gone for water. I saw him take the jerrycan a little while ago."

"Then there is no time to lose, we must leave before he returns," replied the old pastor. Still carrying Shema, even though he was quite a big boy, they left the hut.

Although he was old, the pastor was a strong man. He carried Shema easily and Mama Grace was only just able to keep up with his big strides. He knew the little paths that took them away from the huts, but did not go near the main road or the shops where other eyes might see them and report back to the medicine man if they were questioned. Many people in the area feared the medicine man and dreaded his magic spells and curses.

As they went, Shema begged Mama Grace to tell him how Maji was. He was so afraid that he might have died!

"He's in the hospital with Ishimwe, getting treatment," she reassured Shema. "He was carried there by some of the men from the village, in the ambulance basket, just before I came to find you." Shema was relieved!

Soon they were safe in the house of the pastor. The poor boy was dirty and also very hungry and thirsty. The pastor's wife gave him a bowl of water to wash with, then gave him some delicious porridge and a large cup of fresh, warm milk. It didn't take long for Shema to feel better and he soon found he was singing his little song again, this time, not out of fear, but from happiness! The pastor's wife looked at Shema and her heart went out to him. She wrapped him in a blanket and laid him on her own mattress so that he could sleep in peace; after two bad nights he found he was ready for a nap! While Shema was sleeping the grown-ups prayed and thanked God that they had been able to rescue him before he was harmed by the medicine man and also asked God to show them what to do next, so that he would remain safe.

Mama Grace knew she needed to return to her family as soon as possible. By now they would be worrying about her and she was concerned for them. The pastor and his wife could understand this and they agreed it would be best if she went home at once. They gave her some food and water for the journey and she kissed Shema as he lay sleeping, knowing he would be safe in the pastor's house. The pastor decided that he would wait until it was dark and then bring Shema home on the back of his motorbike. Mama Grace waved goodbye and set out to walk home. Her heart was much lighter than when she had begun her journey!

When Shema first woke up he couldn't think where he was. He felt warm and snug, wrapped in the soft blanket. But then he began to remember what had happened. His body began to tremble and whatever he did, he couldn't lie still. He started to call out for Mama Grace. When the pastor's wife heard Shema calling, she rushed into the bedroom.

"It's all right, Shema," she reassured him. "You are safe here with us. Mama Grace has gone home to Sam and the Old People, but you needed to rest after your ordeal. Tonight my husband will take you back home, too, on his motorbike!" She took Shema into her arms and gave him a hug. Big tears began to come into his eyes and fall down his cheeks. He felt ashamed to cry, but it was so nice to be hugged! He vaguely remembered when his mother was alive and had hugged him. That was before the terrible time when the soldiers had come and taken his mummy and daddy away and they had never come back. In the back of his mind he could remember the screams and guns and running and running and running with Ishimwe and Maji. Sometimes the running would come back to him in a nightmare and he would wake up trembling with fear.

Now he looked up into the kind face of the old lady who was hugging him and somehow he knew that she understood he was not being a baby and it was all right to cry. The tears just came and came and the pastor's wife just hugged and hugged. It made Shema feel better and very safe.

Late that afternoon they all sat down together for a meal. Shema could hardly believe his eyes when he saw meat on his plate. What a treat! His plate was filled with so many good things! He felt that he wanted to save some and take it home for his brother and sister and shyly asked the pastor and his wife if he could do that. They looked at each other and gently shook their heads. "This is for you, now, Shema," said the pastor. "You must eat well and gain strength. We will give you some food for your family that is not cooked, it will keep better. Your sister is at the hospital with your little brother, but she will be glad of the food when she comes home!"

"Thank you so much!" replied Shema. "You are so kind. I have never known anyone so kind except Mama Grace and I think there is a man called Mister God, too. People have told me he loves me, but I haven't met him yet. I sometimes find myself talking to him and I asked him to help me when I was in the medicine man's hut."

"He did help you, too, didn't he?" said the old lady. "He sent Mama Grace to find you and brought her to us to help rescue you!"

"Do you know him?" asked Shema. "I so want to meet him and say thank you." The old lady drew Shema on to her lap. It was a big lap and very comfortable.

"Let me try to explain to you about God, our Father," she said and began to tell him some of the Christian story.

NINE

The Hospital

While Shema was having all these adventures, Ishimwe was at the hospital. Maji was barely alive when he was carried down the hill in the basket-stretcher. At the hospital, Ishimwe was surprised to see so many people everywhere, all sick and waiting for help. Ishimwe had never been to a hospital before, but the men who had carried Maji seemed to know exactly what to do and where to go. She followed them as they carried the sick boy into a large room. A nurse lifted him from the basket and laid him on one of the beds. "This boy is very ill," she chided. "Why have you left it so long to bring him? Where are his parents?"

"I am his sister and we have no parents, we are orphans," explained Ishimwe. "I had no money to bring him; even now I only have a few francs which I have been given. I hope it is enough to cure him!" Ishimwe felt close to tears. She had done all she could, but how could a twelve-year-old girl know what to do?

"Don't worry about the money," said the nurse, a little more kindly, as she realised the situation. "Tell me how long your brother has been sick and what you have done for him."

Ishimwe began to explain how she had spent all she had at the clinic to buy malaria medicine, because she thought that was the cause of the sickness and how they had given him boiled water to drink and bathed his body with cool water.

"You have done very well," the nurse praised her. "You did all the right things. Maybe one day you will be a nurse!"

Ishimwe smiled a shy smile. "How I would like that! But I have not been to school since the war, when mummy and daddy were taken away and killed, along with all my aunts, uncles and grandparents. Now I have my two young brothers to take care of." The nurse sighed. She had heard sad stories like this one, too often. She finished her examination of Maji and explained to Ishimwe that she was going to put a needle into his arm, attached to a tube, so that medicines and fluids could get into his body quickly. Then when the doctor was free, he would come to see her brother. She told Ishimwe that she would have to stay in the hospital to look after Maji; she could sleep under her brother's bed and there were places to wash and cook food just outside the ward.

Ishimwe looked around the room. She had been so worried about Maji that she had been only vaguely aware of the other people in and around the beds. All the patients were children and most of them had tubes in their arms, too. Some beds even had two children lying on them!

Their mothers were taking care of the children, or

talking together. One of them beckoned to Ishimwe to come and talk.

"Are you all right, my dear?" she asked kindly.

"Yes, thank you. I think so. At least my brother is now getting help." The lady could see how very ill Maji was and tried to distract Ishimwe by talking to her.

"Come with me and I will show you where the bathroom is and also where we can cook food." She took Ishimwe on a tour of the ward and grounds.

"Have you any food with you?" she asked.

"No, I'm afraid not," answered Ishimwe. "We came so quickly and also all my money is to pay for treatment."

"Don't worry," said the kind lady, "you can share what I cook until you are able to do your own. Your brother will not need food until he is better. The tube will feed him."

Later in the day the doctor came to see Maji. He shook his head as he examined him. He called Ishimwe over. "Is this your little brother?" he asked gently.

"Yes, sir," whispered Ishimwe shyly, looking up at the man in the white coat.

"I have to tell you that he is very, very ill. We may not be able to save him. Even if we do, the fever may have damaged his brain. He has malaria, just as you thought, but it is the type that affects the brain. We call it cerebral malaria. I understand from the nurse that you have done a good job in looking after him and that you have no parents. I want to tell you not to worry about paying for your treatment. We have a fund that helps orphans and I will make sure it pays for your brother. We will do our best with his treatment; the best thing you can do now is to pray for him."

Ishimwe didn't know what to say or think. She looked at the grave face of the doctor and wondered if she could tell him she didn't know about praying, except the little things Shema had said about "Mister God".

When she thought about Shema, she was worried about him too. Was he all right? Mama Grace had been so worried when she learnt he had gone to the medicine man. He was such a brave boy. Somewhere her heart was crying, "Please don't let me lose my brothers!"

The doctor walked away and Ishimwe sat on the floor by Maji's bed, her head in her hands. The world seemed such a terrible place to be in just now. She closed her eyes, struggling not to cry. Only a few weeks ago she had been so happy with her two brothers, wearing her new sweater. How quickly it had all changed!

She felt an arm around her shoulders and Ishimwe opened her eyes and looked up. The kind mother who had offered her food was sitting next to her on the floor, trying to comfort her. Ishimwe leant against her and felt her kindness flowing into her own body and giving her strength.

"The doctor suggested that you pray," said the kind lady. "Why don't we do that?"

"I don't know how to, what is praying?" sobbed Ishimwe.

"It's talking to our Maker, the Father God," explained the lady. "He made us, he loves us and nothing is too hard for him. Even though you cannot see him, he is there, longing for you to talk to him, longing to be a Father to you. He promises to be a Father to the orphans. Just talk to him as you would your own daddy if he were alive." From somewhere deep inside her heart, Ishimwe found some words.

"Mister God, be a Father to me and the boys. Make Maji well and keep Shema safe, please, please, please!"

The lady next to her said, "Amen." That meant "let it be so". She turned to Ishimwe and smiled. "Now, try not to worry all the time. Let Father take the worry. You come and eat and then sleep." Sleep seemed the last thing Ishimwe thought she would be able to do and she didn't feel hungry either, but she wanted to please this kind lady. Somehow, though, she found that her prayer had made her feel comforted and more peaceful and less alone and scared.

The food tasted so good and as she began to eat, Ishimwe realised that it was ages since she had last eaten a meal and she was very hungry. Afterwards she helped the lady wash the dishes, then she went to the tap and washed herself. When she came back into the ward, she looked at Maji, still unconscious, but looking so peaceful. She lay down to sleep wrapped in a cloth lent to her by the nurse and soon drifted off. The kind mother looked at the sleeping girl and the sick boy and prayed her own prayers for this sad family. She looked at her own daughter in her cot and thanked God that she was getting stronger and thanked God for the doctors and nurses who had worked so hard to make the children well. Then she, too, lay down and slept.

The next morning, when the nurse came to take Maji's temperature she shook her head. It was still far too high! He was still unconscious and every now and then his whole body shook with convulsions. The medicine was still going into his body through the drip, but it didn't seem to be working very well. When the doctor came to do his rounds, he, too, stood at the end of the bed and when he saw the charts, he looked grave. He had hoped that by now Maji would have been getting better. He turned to Ishimwe and told her, "Your little brother is still very sick. We are doing our best. I'm sorry, there is nothing else we can do, except pray." Fighting her tears, Ishimwe looked at the doctor.

"I have asked God to be our Father and to make him better, I am sure he will soon wake up."

"He may wake up in heaven, my dear," the doctor replied. "Sometimes that is the way God answers, for he always knows what is best." Ishimwe turned and looked at the mother who had been so kind. She smiled at the girl.

"Try to be brave, my dear, and don't give up hope. I am going to make some nice hot tea, come and join me for a cup." She took Ishimwe's arm and led her outside the ward to the charcoal fire where a pan of water was boiling. They sat down and Ishimwe felt the strong arm around her. She decided she would speak to God again. It was wonderful to think she had a Father who cared about her and would help her.

"Father God, thank you that you love me and want to help me. Please, I don't want Maji to wake up in heaven. I am sure it is a wonderful place, but I want my little brother here with me. I am not very brave, please help me, Amen."

TEN

Shema's Return

Shema's day passed quickly in the home of the pastor and his wife. Once it grew dark, the pastor's wife made up a bundle of food in a cloth for Shema to give Ishimwe. She tied it on the back of the motorbike, gave Shema a big hug and promised that she would come one day and visit him in his village.

Shema was rather a small boy to travel on the motorbike, so the old pastor decided to put him in front, so that he could hold the handlebars. The pastor had a crash helmet, but Shema's head was too small for him to wear the one he kept for passengers. He told him that he must hold on very tight, particularly when the road was bumpy. Even though the Highway Code allowed passengers to ride in this way, the pastor didn't want any accidents! Shema was very excited. He had always wanted to ride on a motorbike; up until now he had only ever been on a push bike and that was as a passenger. What an adventure! And in the dark, too! He felt very safe with these kind people who had given him wonderful food and truly cared for him.

They set off, travelling really quite slowly over the muddy tracks in the village. It was bumpy and noisy, but Shema found that it was fun to bump up and down! He held on very tightly to the handlebars. They left the village and began climbing the hill. How much faster it was than walking! It was cool at night, too. Sometimes the noise of the engine disturbed an animal or bird and they saw it scuttle off into the bushes. At home, Shema would have been scared in case it was a hyena or a monkey, but now, on the motorbike, he felt no fear!

It seemed no time at all before they saw the lights in the houses of Ruga village. The pastor took Shema straight to Mama Grace's house. "Putt, putt, putt," the little engine purred before it ground to a stop. The door opened and out rushed Sam, followed quickly by his mother.

"Welcome, welcome," cried Mama Grace as the pastor lifted Shema off the motorbike. "Come in!"

"Thank you," said the old pastor. "I will not stay long but I would like to talk to you for a few minutes. We need to make plans to be sure this young man will remain safe."

"Hello, Shema," Mama Grace greeted him with a big smile, as the pastor lifted him off the motorbike.

"Hello Mama Grace, is Maji all right?"

"He is still in the hospital, but I will take you to see him tomorrow," promised Mama Grace. The two boys ran into the house. By now Shema was longing to tell Sam all about his adventures. So much had happened since they last met! He told him about the journey, then about the medicine man's hut. The very thought of it made Shema shake a little with fear. It had been so horrible! Then he told Sam all about the rescue and the kind pastor's wife and finally, about the journey home on the motorbike. Then Sam wanted to hear it all again! What an amazing escape it had been!

The pastor meanwhile talked to Mama Grace. What could be done to help these orphans? He knew that Shema was still at risk of recapture. The medicine man might come to Patrick and demand that Shema be given back to him. Patrick would be too scared not to tell his cousin where Shema lived, in case his cousin worked evil magic against him. Almost everyone was scared of the power of a bad medicine man. They simply could not let Shema go back to his own house and stay there alone, he would just not be safe.

Mama Grace promised to keep Shema at her house with Sam while Ishimwe was in the hospital with Maji, but she knew she could not have all three children living with her forever. Even though it was very late, they called in the Old People, Mama Grace's mother and father and the four of them closed their eyes and asked God to give them wisdom to know what to do for the best.

After that, the pastor gave Mama Grace the food for Ishimwe and went to say goodbye to Shema before starting back on his journey home. "Shema," he said, "never forget that God, *Imana*, loves you and is a Father to you, even though you cannot see him. Always talk to him. Ask him to help you and protect you and obey Mama Grace while you live in her house, for she is a good woman and wants only to help you."

"Yes, sir," he replied, "I promise I will do those things. I want to thank you so much for rescuing me and taking care of me and letting me ride on your motorbike."

The old pastor hugged Shema and hurried out of the house. They heard the "putt, putt, putt" of the bike getting fainter and fainter as he rode away.

"Well, Shema," said Mama Grace, "can you share Sam's mattress tonight? Then tomorrow we will go and see Ishimwe and Maji in the hospital."

"Yes, Mama Grace," he replied. "I would like to do that." After they had eaten a snack of little sweet bananas and had a drink of milk, the boys settled down to sleep. After all his adventures, Shema fell fast asleep very quickly. Mama Grace looked at the two boys sleeping side by side, smiled and said "thank you" to God for them both.

As soon as it was light Sam and Shema were up and outside splashing around in a big basin of cold water, washing. It was much more fun washing when you could pour cold water over each other! When they were dressed they set off together to the well to collect the day's supply of water. So much had happened since the last time Shema went to collect water! It seemed ages ago, not just a few days. The two boys ran down the hill, laughing and chasing each other. It was easy with the empty yellow cans!

Coming back was much more difficult, because the water was heavy, but Sam wanted to hear all about Shema's adventure again, so the time went quickly. As they approached the village, Shema heard some goats bleating and he instantly recognised their voices! They were Patrick's flock. He looked around and saw another small boy was tending them.

"Why are you looking after Patrick's goats?" he asked the lad.

"Patrick has given me the job of goatherd," he replied. "His last goatherd went away and Patrick said when he didn't come back after a day, maybe he will not return, so he gave me the job." Shema's heart sank. He had forgotten about Patrick and now he realised that he could still be in danger; perhaps the medicine man would come to Patrick and find out where he was and take him back to his horrible huts! He also realised that he had lost his job and now had no way of earning money to help Ishimwe buy food.

ELEVEN

Turning the Corner

"Let's go to your home quickly," Shema said to Sam. He wanted to talk to Mama Grace because he felt afraid again. The boys carried the water as quickly as they were able, back to Sam's home. Mama Grace had been making them some millet porridge, so they sat down on the back door step to eat it. It was lovely to have a hot breakfast and Shema made it last as long as possible. Then he went to talk to Sam's mum.

"I am frightened, Mama Grace," Shema explained and told her about meeting the boy who was now taking care of Patrick's goats. Mama Grace looked thoughtful.

"I can understand your worry," she said. "I think we need to talk to someone wise like the pastor of our church. Meanwhile, stay close to me and near the house." After they had finished breakfast Sam collected his exercise book and pencil and went off skipping, to school. Shema helped Mama Grace tidy the compound and prepare food for the Old People and also some more food to take to the hospital for Ishimwe. Then they started their journey to visit Maji. It was a very long walk, but Shema didn't mind. He felt safe alongside Sam's mum and he was so excited about seeing his sister and little brother again that the time went quickly.

There were many people at the hospital and everyone seemed so busy. At first they didn't know who to ask about Maji. Eventually they saw a nurse who was able to tell them how to find the children's ward. As they walked through the door the first thing they saw was a group of doctors and nurses standing around a bed. Near them was Ishimwe, looking tired, but with a happy smile on her face.

One of the doctors was telling the others, "This child is a miracle. He seemed to be dying and nothing we did was helping him, then this morning his temperature started to come down and he has become conscious again!"

The doctors moved on to see the next child and Ishimwe suddenly saw that Mama Grace and Shema had entered the ward. She ran over and hugged them both, laughing at one moment, then crying the next! "Maji's going to be all right!" she told them. "Everyone said he was dying and I should say goodbye to him, but Mister God heard me when I asked him to make Maji better!"

Shema went to look at his little brother and Maji returned his smile. Then Shema turned to Ishimwe. "I, too, had some bad problems at the house of the medicine man and asked Mister God to rescue me and he did. I have been talking to him, too."

Mama Grace was talking to the mother who had helped Ishimwe and was thanking her. She told her about the three children and how hard life was for them. Mama Grace also told her about the terrible experience Shema had when he went to the medicine man for help.

The two ladies decided to pray together because they both knew that the children still needed help and protection. Mama Grace then went to talk to the nurse who was caring for Maji and found out that if he continued to get well, he would be able to return home in a couple of days!

She knew that she had to find some way of helping this family and very soon. "Come along, Shema," called Mama Grace. "We need to go home now. Say goodbye to Ishimwe and Maji. They will soon be back home with you!" Shema was about to complain and say he wanted to stay longer when he remembered his promise to the kind pastor who had brought him home. So he did as he was told and they began the long walk back to the village.

"Before we go home I want to go and visit the pastor of my church," Mama Grace told him. "I want to tell him of your worries about Patrick and see what he can suggest." The pastor lived in a small house on a hill. When they arrived he was not at home, but his wife took them in and made them a cup of tea. She was sure he would not be long. After drinking his cup of tea Shema went outside to play with the small children of the family. They were singing a song and Shema recognised it at once as the one he had learnt sitting outside the school. "God is so good, God is so good, God is so good, He's so good to me!" they sang. He joined in with great gusto. He knew the words were true, God is good! The song also reminded Shema of the teacher who had said he would pray that Shema could go to school.

"Mister God," whispered Shema, a bit shyly, "you rescued me and have made Maji better, so I know it is true that you love me. Please could I ask you for something else? I really, really want to go to school so that one day I can be an airline pilot!"

Meanwhile, inside the house, Mama Grace was talking to the pastor's wife and soon the pastor returned and joined them. She told them the whole story of all that had happened to the three children. She explained her fear that Shema could be kidnapped and taken back to the medicine man's house. She would like to take care of all the children, but she knew she could not do that, with her own two children and her elderly parents to care for. What could be done?

The pastor sat and listened to all Mama Grace had to say. He looked very thoughtful. "I think you are right to be worried," he said, "but I also think we may have some answers to these problems. I have heard only recently about a village which is being built near here. It is called "Village of Hope", with little houses in it for orphans who have no relatives to take care of them. I know there are many such families and they may have to wait until a house is available, but I shall certainly see if their names can be put on the list. It is a really good, safe place, with supervision from caring people and opportunities for the children to go to school and to lead more normal lives. However, that will be for the future. Just now I think we should go to see the policeman in the village. He is a very good and honest man and has helped me several times when I have needed him to protect vulnerable people. If he knows the situation and is willing to visit Shema and Ishimwe each day, I don't think Patrick's cousin would dare to hurt or kidnap Shema. If the authorities catch a medicine man using a child as a servant he will be sent to prison at once and locked up for a very long time. Yes, I think we should go at once and talk to the police, let's go right away!"

"Thank you for your advice and help, Pastor," nodded Mama Grace. Then she went into the garden. "Shema," she called, "it's time to go! We are going to call in at the police station on our way home, so that we can explain to the policeman all the troubles you have had. The pastor is coming with us!"

Shema quickly said good bye to the pastor's children he was playing with and joined Mama Grace and the pastor. The three of them walked down a small hill and into the village. There they went into the little hut that served as a police station. Shema felt a bit scared as he had never talked to a policeman before and this one looked so important in his uniform! The policeman knew the pastor and respected him, so when he told Shema's story to him, the police officer took it very seriously. He looked at the small boy and smiled at him.

"Now, don't you worry any more, young man," he said. "Stay with Mama Grace at her house until your sister returns, then, when you are ready to go home, come and tell me first. I shall come to visit you every morning and every evening. Patrick's cousin will be far too scared of going to prison to frighten you again!"

This made Shema feel much better and he skipped all the rest of the way back to Sam's home.

Sam was waiting for him. He told him all about his day at school and showed Shema his exercise book. They looked at the letters and Sam began to teach Shema the alphabet. This made Shema so excited! Sam promised to teach him some numbers too, another time, but it was getting dark and was time for bed. As the boys washed their dusty feet and prepared for bed, Shema felt that things were going to be better for him and maybe, just maybe, he was nearer his dream of going to school and perhaps one day he would indeed be an airline pilot! He stretched his arms out wide and zoomed around the room, pretending to be an aeroplane. Soon, Sam joined in the game and they made so much noise that Mama Grace came to see what they were doing. She laughed when she saw the two boys twirling around. It was so good to see them happy and playing like young boys should. She, too, felt very relieved that the policeman would keep a watch on Shema.

The next day was warm and sunny. It felt good to Shema to feel warm again and to be able to play outside. Mama Grace's parents also were glad to see the sun. They were old and complained that their bones ached when it was cold and wet. Now the sun was shining they wanted to start planting beans in the garden. Shema took a hoe and went to help them. He liked to dig the red earth and plant the beans. It always surprised him how quickly they grew into strong plants. He liked being with the Old People, because they always had many stories to tell of how life was in Rwanda years ago. They remembered the time when wild animals lived in the bush, but now there were only a few monkeys and hyenas, for all the large wild animals now lived only in the game park. Sam's grandfather told Shema how he used to look after the goats, like most other boys and how his father had once found him in the kitchen and had scolded him. Boys did not help in the kitchen, they looked after the animals, he was told! In those days very few children went to school and even now, the Old People could not write their names, but had to sign forms by using their thumb print. Shema thought that was fun and began to practise making a thumb print in the mud. He promised himself, however, that one day soon, he would write his own name. Perhaps Sam would teach him after school that very day!

Later in the day, Mama Grace decided that she and Shema would go to his house and see if it needed to be tidied up ready for Ishimwe to bring Maji back home. They walked up the hill together and Shema found he was shivering a little as they went past Patrick's house. Mama Grace looked at him and put her arm around his shoulder.

"Don't worry," she said. "Remember that God loves you and will take care of you."

"Yes, I'll try," he answered. The house was damp inside where the rain had leaked through the roof and there were puddles on the floor. Mama Grace sighed to herself. The house really was in a tumble-down state. No wonder the children became sick! She silently asked God to take care of them until a good house became available for them in the Village of Hope.

TWELVE

The Policeman Visits

Mama Grace and Shema worked hard to make the house look as neat as possible and they put the food they had been given into the store cupboard. It was almost time to go back as Sam was due home from school, when they heard footsteps. For a moment both Mama Grace and Shema went quiet and stayed still, wondering who was around. When they saw the face of the policeman in the doorway they felt so relieved!

"I decided to start coming right away," explained the policeman with a big smile, "to make sure that nobody steals anything from the house and to show Patrick that I am around!"

"Thank you," said Shema. "That is very kind of you."

"I was wondering," continued the police officer, "as you are no longer a goatherd, if you would do a little work for my wife?"

"I am sure I can," answered Shema, almost breathless with surprise. "I am big and strong and work very hard!"

"I need someone big and strong to sweep my yard each day and I am so busy that I cannot always hoe my garden. My wife cannot manage these jobs. Would you help me? I will pay you, of course."

"I would love to do that!" exclaimed Shema, hardly daring to believe his ears. "I can start tomorrow, what time should I come?"

"I don't mind what time you come, as long as you come each day. Do you go to school? You could come after school if you like and when you have finished, I will bring you home, so that you need not fear walking up the hill alone."

"I don't go to school, but I very much want to because when I am grown up I want to be an airline pilot!"

"That sounds a wonderful idea," said the policeman. "Don't let anyone make fun of you or steal your dream. That's settled then. I'll expect you tomorrow about the time when the children come home from school."

Then the policeman turned to Mama Grace, who was beaming all over her face, she was so happy for Shema. Her pastor had told her that the policeman was a good man, so she had no concerns about the job.

"Will Shema's sister and brother return tomorrow?" the policeman asked.

"I think so," Mama Grace replied. "And thank you for your kindness to this boy. He is a good boy and will work well."

"My wife is sick and she is too weak to do all the work. I am busy, so we really do need a boy to help. I promise, we will treat him well. I, too, was an orphan. I understand how very hard it can be. I am glad he has dreams for his future. I hope he will be able to go to school."

The three of them walked back down into the village and as they passed Patrick's house, Mama Grace was sure she saw the man scuttle quickly inside. She was glad if he had seen the policeman escorting them!

Sam was waiting for them at his house, football in hand. "Come and play!" he called to his friend.

"I'd love to," Shema said, "but I have lots of news to tell you and I want you to teach me how to write my name. Can you do that?"

"Oh yes, that will be easy, but come and play first!" As they walked to the bare field of brown earth that served them as a football pitch, Shema told Sam about his new job.

"Wow, that sounds great!" said Sam. "You could save up your money and come to school with me!"

"I can't do that," replied Shema, shaking his head. "Ishimwe will need it all for food."

"We could do something," said Sam, suddenly excited. "We could go to school and ask my teacher how much it costs. Let's go up there now and see if he's around!"

Shema thought that was a great idea, so the boys walked up the dusty track enjoying the late afternoon sunshine. They were very near the school when they heard a sudden noise on the path right in front of them. Both boys froze in fear. A big, black, poisonous snake was right in their way! They had no stick in their hands to club it and just didn't know what to do. They couldn't go forwards and if they moved quickly to turn round, it might strike at them!

They wanted to shout out, "help!" but their voices had disappeared and they were afraid to move or even take their eyes off the snake. Briefly, glancing down at his feet, Shema saw a large stone. If only he could pick it up before the snake struck . . . but if he moved to get it, would the snake go for him? And even if he managed to throw the stone at the snake's head, would it kill it, or would it become so angry that he would get bitten or spat at? The venom, he knew, could kill him. When he had been looking after the goats, once or twice he had seen little snakes and driven them off by waving his stick, but he had never seen one as big as this and this time he had no stick with him. It seemed to the boys that they stood completely still for ages, silently looking at the snake, who was looking at them, rearing its great head ready to strike.

"Mister God, help me again," Shema whispered in his head. It was really up to him to do something; he had chased off small snakes before as a goatherd. Sam probably had never had to do that, he thought to himself. As quickly and quietly as he could, he grasped the stone and hurled it at the snake's head. "Don't let me miss, don't let me miss," he silently prayed.

The stone hit the snake right between the eyes. It hissed in fury, but could not see to spit its poison at the boys and had received such a blow that it then keeled over. Quickly, both boys grabbed other stones and threw them at the snake, to make sure it was mortally injured and would die. Then they ran as fast as their legs would carry them, over to the school building. They pushed the door of the first classroom, and were so relieved to find that it was open, they almost fell inside.

"Hey, what's this all about?" a voice asked them. The boys managed to find their voices at last.

"It's a snake, a huge, black, spitting cobra!" It was dark in the classroom, as the teacher had just put the shutters over the windows for the night, but Shema recognised the teacher as the one who had spoken kindly to him about attending school all those weeks ago.

"Where is the snake?" asked the teacher.

"Just on the path outside, we think we may have killed it," said Sam.

"Well, I had better go and check," said the teacher, picking up a very big club from beside his desk. "A wounded animal is a dangerous one. You stay in here, while I go and investigate."

THIRTEEN

Dead Snake

In a few minutes the teacher was back. "You are right. The snake you hit is a really big, spitting black cobra and I'm happy to say that it is quite dead. You have been very brave and also sensible," he went on to say. "Well done! If that snake had been near the goats, it would have eaten one, or if it had been near the infants' class, a child could have died. Those snakes even kill lions when they lash out, spitting their venom. However did you manage to kill it before it killed you?"

The teacher could see the boys were really quite shocked now that the danger was over. "Come and sit down," he suggested. The teacher went to his desk and pulled out two bottles of cola and gave them to the boys. "This will make you feel better."

"It was Shema that got the stone and hit its head," Sam explained, sitting at one of the desks. Shema was trembling with shock, now that the danger was over. A spitting black cobra is feared more than any other snake, because it can kill so easily, especially if it has been surprised or cornered by humans.

"Tell me about it," requested the teacher. He knew the best way to calm Shema was to allow him to talk about what happened. Shema and Sam were glad of the sweet cola to drink; it was a rare treat for them.

Between sips, Shema told the teacher about the stone
by his feet and how he had asked God to help him to
pick it up and throw it before the cobra spat at him,
and to help him hit the snake's head.

The teacher looked thoughtfully at Shema. "You
are not one of our pupils, are you?" he asked, "But
your face is a face I know!"

Shema told the teacher that he had been the
goatherd who liked to come close to the school and
hear the lessons the children were learning.

"I remember now!" the teacher exclaimed. "You
are the boy who wants to go to school; I have done
what I said and from time to time I have been praying
that God would make a way for you, even though it
seems impossible."

"A lot has happened since you spoke to me that
day," said Shema with a shy smile. "When you said
God loved me, I did not understand and did not
know who Mister God was and had no idea what you
meant when you said to pray. Then, things began to
happen to me and I began to talk to Mister God and
he has helped me."

"I am very interested," said the teacher with a
smile. "Please tell me your story!" Shema began to
tell him about the sweaters, about Maji's illness and
about the medicine man, with Sam butting in every
now and then to confirm the story. Shema ended up
telling him about the policeman and his new job and
even that Sam was going to teach him how to write
his name.

"I am in Primary 3 of this school," Sam piped up. "If I pass my end of year exam I will come into your class!"

"I will look forward to that," the teacher replied. "I can see you are a good friend to Shema." He turned to Shema. "You have done a very good turn for this school, because you were so brave and killed a snake that could have done great harm to my pupils. I would like to help you. If you really want to learn so very much, then I will teach you. Come here each day after school has finished and I will give you a lesson and start to teach you to read. It will be for about half an hour, then you can go to do your work for the policeman's wife. Does that sound a good idea?"

"Oh sir!" Shema could hardly find the words in his excitement. "Oh yes, please!"

"It is getting late now and I think you boys should get home or Sam's mother will worry that something bad has happened to you," the teacher continued. "I will walk with you to your village and talk to Sam's mother and also to the policeman, so that they both know who I am and that I am genuinely going to help you. I also want to tell them how very brave you boys have been. I am so glad you are learning to love and trust God, it is the best thing you can ever do in your life."

They all got up and the teacher locked up the classroom. Outside on the path, a little crowd had gathered by the dead snake. "Look at this snake," the people were saying, "What a big one! Thank goodness it has been killed before it killed someone!"

"Yes," said the teacher, "and this is the brave young man who killed it!" The people turned to look at Shema.

"Oh and he's just a small lad," they said, shaking their heads in amazement. "You must be very brave!"

Shema, Sam and the teacher walked down the hill to Sam's home and the boys couldn't wait to introduce the kind teacher to Mama Grace and to tell the story of the spitting black cobra. Mama had to hear it, then the Old People and they all shook their heads in amazement. Mama Grace made tea for the teacher and the boys went into the yard to play while the grown-ups talked.

Next the teacher walked over to the police station to talk to the officer there. The policeman was happy for Shema to have a reading class before he came to do his work, or for him to do the jobs at other times of the day. The two men talked about the dangers to young children from evil men like the medicine man and how they could prevent such things happening in their area. The teacher decided he must talk to all the children in his school and warn them about such evil people.

The next day, Sam and Shema were the centre of attention, because the news had spread throughout the village that they had managed to kill a spitting black cobra! They were heroes! As they went together to the well to collect the water, they were asked to tell the story over and over again. People were so amazed, that it made Shema realise more and more how much God had helped him, because it was a miracle that they were alive and the snake dead and not the other way around!

Once they had taken the water to Mama Grace, Sam had to go on his way to school. Shema didn't mind too much that he was not able to go with his friend, because today they were going to the hospital and if he was strong enough Maji was going to be allowed to come home.

First, he and Mama Grace took some water to the house on the hill, ready for Ishimwe. The Old Lady was busy pounding some millet for the children. They also had some rice and beans to take to the house. It would all be such a surprise for Ishimwe, it made Shema smile just to think of how amazed she would be!

It was a long walk to the hospital, but this time, when they arrived, they knew where to find Maji. He was running around the ward, looking like his old self, making the other children laugh. Ishimwe had gathered her things into a small bundle and was saying goodbye to the mother who had helped her so much. This mother had taught her about God and how to pray to him and Ishimwe would never forget that. She looked at her small brother and thanked God again for the miracle that he was alive and well.

Then she saw Shema and Mama Grace and ran to give them a hug!

"I am so pleased to see you, Shema and you too, Mama Grace," she said. Everyone smiled, then Mama Grace looked at Maji.

"How well you look now!" she exclaimed.

"I want to go home!" said Maji.

"That is why we are here, to take you home," explained Mama Grace. "But first, I need to see the nurse." The three children waited while she went to the nurses' office. Her pastor had given her some money from the church, so that the hospital bill could be paid. This, along with the money from the orphans' fund, meant that Ishimwe didn't have to pay anything! She was so grateful.

Very soon, the four of them set out on the way home. Because Maji was only five years old and had been so ill, Mama Grace had also brought money for them all to go home on a bus. What excitement that caused! Maji had never been in a bus or a car in his whole life and it was a long time since Shema had ridden in one. Ishimwe's eyes just shone with happiness and appreciation.

FOURTEEN

Back Together Again

On the bus, Shema told Maji about his ride on the motorbike. The little boy wanted to hear the story over and over again. Shema was so pleased to see him that he didn't mind having to repeat the story. He wanted to tell him about the snake too, but thought perhaps it would be boasting to do so.

When the bus reached the village, they all got off and walked first to Mama Grace's house. There they were greeted and hugged by the Old People. A hot meal was waiting for them all, it was a feast! There was cassava, rice, beans and a meat stew! It was like Christmas and birthdays all rolled into one! It was wonderful to have people care for them and the children were very grateful. Shema was restless, though. He wanted to take Ishimwe up the hill to their own house and to see her face when she saw the stash of food in her little cupboard there!

Maji was strong enough to walk up to their own house. Indeed, he skipped and ran some of the way. Ishimwe was so happy when she saw the food waiting for them, and everything as nice as it could be in the house.

"I have one more surprise," said Mama Grace. "We have bought you mosquito nets! Shema will help me fix them over your mattresses and then, you must sleep under them every night. It should help you not to get malaria again." Mosquito nets are made of a very fine net material and hang from the ceiling, but are long enough to tuck under the mattress. They are sprayed with a strong chemical which is harmless to people, but which mosquitoes hate. The holes in the net are too small for mosquitoes to enter, so the person underneath is protected from their bites.

This kindness was too much for Ishimwe. Tears began to roll down her face. "Whatever have we done to deserve all the help you have given us?" she asked Mama Grace.

"You are good children and we are sad that your parents were killed in the war. The Lord God tells us to take care of orphans and because he loves you and we want to obey him, my family are very happy to help you. We are especially pleased that you are learning to love God for yourselves."

Ishimwe smiled. "We didn't know about God before all this happened, but we want to know more and more and I promise I will come with my brothers to church on Sundays." Shema was pleased when he heard this. He was so glad that he didn't have to take care of the goats any more; he did miss them a bit, but now he was free on Sundays and could go with Sam and learn more about Mister God!

While the boys went outside to play, Mama Grace told Ishimwe all about Shema's escape from the medicine man and how the policeman would call each day to make sure all was well. She also told Ishimwe about the snake, about Shema's new job helping the policeman's wife and about the teacher's promise to give Shema a lesson every day. She assured Ishimwe that the policeman and the teacher were good people who could be trusted. "You have many new friends now, Ishimwe. When you are worried, afraid or have problems, you must come and talk to us. We want to help you as much as we can. My pastor is also finding out about some new, good houses which are being built for families like yours by a charity that cares for orphans. Don't get too excited yet, but perhaps one day in the future, you all may be able to move to somewhere safe and new with no leaky roof!"

Shema and Maji had been playing tag in the garden. It was lovely to hear Maji's laughter again, but Ishimwe had been told by the doctor that Maji would still need to rest, so she called the boys to come in.

"Maji, it is time for you to go and rest. You can go under the net for the very first time!" Maji was excited about that and went at once to lie down.

"Shema," continued Ishimwe, "Mama Grace has told me about the medicine man and the snake. I am so proud of you! She also told me that the teacher and the policeman both want to help you. I am very pleased and will do all I can to help, too. So, if you are going today for a lesson, you had better go to the school right now! But please come in to me before

you go on to work at the policeman's house, so that I
know you are all right."

"Yes, of course, and thank you," said Shema, as he
ran out of the house and began to run to school. How
much had happened since yesterday when he had
gone there with Sam to play football! He laughed to
himself, because they never did play that game!

Shema reached the school just in time to see the
children leaving the classrooms and going home,
carrying their exercise books on their heads. Some
children were kicking a ball made of plastic bags and
twine, such as he and Sam used when they played
football. Just outside the school he saw the remains
of the snake and many ants crawling over it and
having a very good dinner out of what was left! There
beside it was the large stone. Shema shuddered when
he saw it, remembering his fear, and how he had
nearly been spat at by the cobra. "Thank you Mister
God, for helping me," he quietly whispered, now
understanding that although he could not see anyone,
God could see him and loved him and wanted to help
him. "Thank you, too, for the teacher who will help
me learn. One day, I will be a pilot, I promise you! I
will be the best pilot in the whole, wide world!"

Shema waited until all the children had gone and
then he respectfully knocked on the door of the
classroom into which he and Sam had fled the day
before. "Come in!" called the friendly voice of the
teacher. "Good, good, I am glad you have come,
Shema."

So Shema had his first lesson, beginning to learn the alphabet. He remembered the letters Sam had already taught him and did really well. The teacher praised him. He could see that Shema really wanted to learn and would be a good pupil. "When you have learnt to read well, I will buy you a Bible," he promised Shema. "The Bible is God's word to us and full of wonderful stories. It is the most precious book in all the world!"

"Thank you, sir," said Shema, his eyes shining with surprise and delight. A book of his very own! "I will try as hard as I can!"

"Good boy! Come again tomorrow!" the teacher waved to Shema as he ran off down the path. Just as he had promised, Shema called in and told Ishimwe that he was now on his way to work in the policeman's garden, then ran off to his new job. He felt so happy! He had friends, a good job earning money and was being taught to read. His family were all safely back home again, it was all wonderful!

FIFTEEN

Kind Friends

Shema really had found some good friends. He went every week from Monday to Friday to have his lesson with the teacher. To have a teacher all to himself meant that he could really learn quickly and within just a few weeks Shema was able to read short sentences. He was learning to write, too and was now very proud that he could write his own name very neatly. He was looking forward so much to the day when he could read well enough to have the Bible which had been promised him!

Ishimwe kept her promise and every Sunday she would take her two brothers to the church. They loved the singing and the dancing! Very quickly they learnt the words of the songs and often Ishimwe sang them while she worked in the house and the garden. At the end of each day, just before they went to bed, all three children sang together and then talked to God their Father and thanked him for their new friends and for all the good things that had happened to them in recent weeks.

The pastor kept his promise, too and went to find out more about the Village of Hope which was being built. He met with the project manager and told him all about the children and especially that Shema was in danger. The man promised that he would do all he could to help and showed the pastor the houses that were being built. They were good houses with a living room, two bedrooms and a store room along with an outside toilet and a kitchen. The whole village was neat and tidy and there was a house in the middle which was the home of a social worker who would be an "auntie" and take care of the children if any of them needed any advice or help. There was also a small clinic where they could get medicine and see a nurse if they were sick. The plan was to have sponsors who lived in richer countries who would pay some money each month so that the children could have food, clothes and also go to school. The pastor was impressed with the new village. If Ishimwe, Shema and Maji were able to have a home there, he knew they would have a good future and be well cared for. He, too, had become very fond of the little family who worked so hard and were always so brave and cheerful, and now came regularly to his church.

The policeman also proved to be a good friend to Shema. Shema was a reliable and hard worker. He never complained and was happy to do any job inside or outside the house. The policeman's wife was a sick lady and was so glad to have a young boy to help her with the chores and his sunny smile always cheered her up!

Almost every day after doing her chores, Ishimwe walked with Maji down the hill to the village and called on Mama Grace and the Old People. They were always pleased to see her and had become her friends and advisers. She loved to sit with the Old Lady and hear stories of when she had been young. The Old Man also had many stories to tell. He liked to play with Maji and often while the ladies talked they could hear him and Maji laughing together.

One day Mama Grace began to teach Ishimwe how to sew using her sewing machine and found that Ishimwe was very good at it. "Why, you could earn a living from sewing clothes!" exclaimed Mama Grace.

Ishimwe gasped, "I would love to do that!"

"Well, you can use my machine any time you like," offered Mama Grace. "To start with, make one dress, then sell it for a profit and you can start a little business!"

"Yes, I could," replied Ishimwe thoughtfully. "Then if I earned enough, the boys could go to school!"

"I would be glad to help you with the sewing," said the Old Lady. "I can still cut out patterns and fasten loose threads even though I am old. I would like to be useful."

"Oh, that would be wonderful!" said Ishimwe, as the idea began to take hold in her mind. She had never before thought that she could make a living for herself and the boys. The more she thought about it, the more possible it seemed and she became excited.

"I will start you off," said Mama Grace. "I have a

length of material which I meant to use for a dress for Grace. Now Grace has grown so big I don't think it is enough. You can start and make a child's dress and sell it in the market. You should get enough money to buy another length of material. I'll find the cloth and you can start tomorrow, if you like!"

"Oh thank you!" cried Ishimwe. "I can't wait to tell Shema! He has been such a good boy and worked so hard for such a long time. Perhaps it won't be too long before he can go to school properly. He's doing very well learning his lessons. Do you know, he dreams of being an airline pilot?"

"Oh yes, I know that!" replied Mama Grace, smiling to herself as she remembered the night when Shema and Sam were whirling around the bedroom like aeroplanes!

The dressmaking plan went very well. With Mama Grace's help, Ishimwe soon made her first little skirt. Somebody bought it the very first day she walked to the market to sell it! Very proudly she took the money to the stall where material was sold and bought another, larger piece. It was enough to make a bigger skirt. Soon she learnt how to make a dress. Mama Grace helped her to write down the money from her sales and the money she spent on materials. She was a proper businesswoman and soon had a little money to put into a pot as savings for school fees for the boys!

Each Sunday the three children went to church. They loved to go and began to make more good friends. Ishimwe was in the youth choir and both the boys were in the Sunday School choir. They learnt many songs and loved to sing all the time. They were also learning Bible stories and verses by heart.

The pastor had grown fond of these cheerful little orphans who faced life so bravely. One day he had a visitor call at his house.

"*Hodi!*" (Can I come in?) came a man's voice.

"*Karibu!*" (You're welcome!) the pastor answered. It was the project manager from the Village of Hope!

"Good day, sir," the man greeted the pastor. "I have some very good news for you! The three children about whom you told us a little while ago are now at the top of the list and we have a house for them!"

"That is so wonderful, my friend! Such good news!" replied the pastor.

"I would like to meet the children in their home where they live now, then take them to visit the Village of Hope. Can you arrange such a visit?"

"Of course. I will go and see the children this afternoon and then, if it is convenient with you, they could meet with you this Saturday. There is a widow who has been helping them. She has been like an auntie to them. May she come along too?"

"Of course, that sounds a very good idea!"

After the man had gone, the pastor hurried along to Mama Grace's house to share the good news with her and to ask her to come with him to the children's home. They walked together up the hill and when the pastor saw the tumble-down mud brick house, his smile became even larger. What a wonderful new home these children would have!

SIXTEEN

New Home

Ishimwe was bending over the fire, cooking the evening rice outside in the yard when the visitors arrived. Shema had just returned from helping the policeman's wife and was now washing Maji in a bowl of water. Well, he was supposed to be washing him, but from the splashing and squealing it sounded more like a water fight!

Mama Grace helped to dry Maji and the three children came inside the house to talk to their pastor. Ishimwe apologised to him.

"I am sorry I have not got a soft chair for you to sit on and we have no cola to offer you. Would you like a cup of tea?"

"A cup of tea would be lovely, my dear," he said. "And while we drink it I can tell you the reason for my visit."

Ishimwe went to boil some water and Mama Grace helped her make some sweet, spiced African tea. There was a little milk that she had brought from her cow, so this was added. To have *"chai"* like this was a special treat for them all! There was enough for them all to have a cup each, though they did have to take turns to use the only two plastic mugs in the house!

"I have come with some very good news for you,"

the pastor explained. "There is a new house ready for you in the Village of Hope, if you would like to live there. On Saturday morning the man in charge will come with me to visit you here, then we will all go to see the house. It is not too far away, so you can still visit your friends in our village, come along to our church and Shema can keep his job and get to his lessons at the school too!"

The three children looked at each other and gasped with delight! A new house for them! No more leaky roofs and walls that were falling down! No longer would they be up on the hill with no other house near them. Shema would no longer be in danger! It all sounded almost too good to be true.

Mama Grace looked at Ishimwe with love in her eyes. How she admired this young girl who had been such a good mother to her younger brothers. She was too thin and looked far older than her twelve years. Perhaps even she too could enjoy a little childhood. "I am coming with you to visit the new house," said Mama Grace, "but I will only let you move there if you promise me one thing."

"What is that?" asked Ishimwe.

"You don't forget to come and visit me very often!"

"How could we forget! You are like family to us," promised Ishimwe. "And I would like to still come and sew. Will that be possible even when we are in the new house?"

"Of course!" replied Mama Grace. "Why, we must

get that new dress finished so that you can sell it in the market very soon. You have a good business started, you can't stop now!"

"Well," said the pastor, when the excitement had died down and everyone had drunk their *"chai"*, "I think we need to say thank you to our heavenly Father, who has worked a miracle for you." They all sang a song,

"God will make a way,
Where there seems to be no way.
He works in ways we cannot see,
I know He'll make a way for me,
God will make a way!"

Then they thanked God for all his love and care and for the new house he had provided for the children.

It was hard to wait until Saturday to see the new house! Even before it was really light, Shema was up and dressed and off to the well. Whatever the day, they still had to fetch water! Then, all three children washed and put on their best clothes. For Shema and Ishimwe that meant putting on the sweaters they had been given by Mama Grace and Maji put on the one he had been given when Shema had prayed. The day would probably be too hot for wearing them, but they so wanted to look smart!

Ishimwe made them some tea, even though they felt too excited to drink it! When Mama Grace and Sam appeared, they were longing to start their new adventure. Ishimwe wished the Old People could come with them, but they would not be able to walk that far. Mama Grace promised to tell them all about the new house when she got back home. They all then had to wait for their pastor and the project manager from the charity to arrive at their house. Fortunately, they also came quite quickly.

First of all the children had to sit down with the grown ups and answer all the questions they were asked. The man from the charity had a questionnaire to fill in. This house they were now living in, had it belonged to their parents? Was the land theirs, did it belong to their family? Were any of their relatives alive? The answer to all these questions was "no".

The man then gently asked them what they remembered about their parents and how they died. Ishimwe began to shake as she tried to tell the man all that she had seen and heard on that terrible day. Mama Grace put her arm around the girl. It was hard, but very important that she told her story.

"I think I have all the information I need," said the man eventually. "Now come, let me take you to the new village! There is a house for you there, all ready to move in to, if you want it. There is no rent. It will become your family home. The social worker, Delphine, who lives in the Village of Hope, will want to try to help you and be like an auntie to you, but you will be free to come and go, to visit your friends here in Ruga just as often as you wish. If you want to come, then we are all here to help you when you need it, but we will not interfere in your family life. Above all, we want you to be safe and happy!"

It sounded almost too good to be true! The little group all went out of the house and into the sunshine, then walked through their village, through a banana plantation, down a path and suddenly they saw a block of lovely new houses, all neatly in rows!

First they went to the largest house on the estate, where a very jolly looking young lady appeared. She was the social worker who would be their new "auntie".

"Hello!" she said to the project manager. "Are these the children you told me about?" She looked at Ishimwe, Shema and Maji and smiled broadly. "My name is Delphine. You are very welcome to our Village of Hope! Come, let me get the keys and show you the house we thought you would like!" By now Shema was dancing with excitement! They were going to have one of these nice houses!

Delphine stopped at the house which had a number seven painted on the outside. Shema, Sam and Maji ran in, longing to explore! Shema gasped when he saw the freshly painted doors and window frames and there was even glass in the windows!

The boys ran round all the rooms, then outside to explore the kitchen, toilet and little yard. There was a hedge planted around the house which separated it from the ones each side.

Ishimwe stood with the grown-ups outside, totally overwhelmed! "Is this really for us?" she asked. "We don't have to be your servants to live here?"

Delphine smiled. "Here is the key. If you want this house, it is yours. You are totally free to say 'yes' and live here, or say 'no' and stay where you are. Kind people who live in a land far away have raised money to build these houses for orphans. The only qualification is that you have no relatives left in your family who could take care of you and we know you do not. You are not servants, but I hope we will be friends! I understand that you are starting to sew at Mama Grace's house. That is fine, you can live your lives just how you want to!" Ishimwe looked from one person to the next. Her eyes were full of tears, not of sadness, but of gratitude.

"I can't begin to say thank you enough," she said. "How can anyone say what their heart feels! Mine is bursting with happiness. I promise you, I will keep this house well and be a good mother to my brothers."

"It is us who should say thank you to you," replied Delphine, "for you have taken care of your brothers and done a wonderful job. You deserve this better home!" Just then the boys rushed back outside.

"Come and see, Ishy, come and see," Sam shouted. "There is a hedge, a yard, a super toilet and a real kitchen!"

"The next door house has chickens," chimed in Maji. "Can we keep chickens, too?"

"When can we move in?" asked Shema. He was so excited, he was hopping from one foot to another!

"As soon as you like," replied Delphine, with another of her big beaming smiles.

"Come on, Ishy," begged Shema, "let's go home right now and get our things!" The pastor had been very quiet, just happy to watch the children in their excitement. For the first time he spoke.

"These children have been coming to my church for some months and have learnt to love God and to pray. They even help in the church and sing in the choirs. Our church has a fund to help orphans and widows. I want to buy three new mattresses for them to sleep on. I think we should go to the village store and buy them, then find help to bring everything here. As it is Saturday, we should be able to do it at once!"

"Thank you so much!" chorused the children together. They could not take in all that was happening! This had to be the best day of their lives, ever!

Later that day Ishimwe, Shema and Maji moved into their new home, helped by all their new friends. They wrapped up their few belongings in a *kitenge* cloth and took the few items of furniture, put them on their heads and began to walk to the new house. As they went through the village, several people called out to them and handed the children little gifts of food or household items, to wish them well and help them settle. The whole village had heard the story of the house in the Village of Hope and were very pleased for the children. Had not their beloved country of Rwanda seen so much sadness? Now it was time to help to bring back some happiness. And so the little family moved into a safe, good home.

Now Shema is no longer a poor goatherd without a future! Yes, his prayer was answered and there came the exciting day when he was able to enrol in school! He didn't mind the long walk up the hill, he was used to that. He would not be in the same class as Sam, but he promised himself that he would work so hard that he would one day catch him up!

He still dreams of becoming an airline pilot and who knows? We know, and Shema knows, we have a loving Father God who answers prayers!

Also available from Dernier Publishing:

Deepest Darkness
by Denise Hayward

Ten-year-old Abi suffers from terrible nightmares. On holiday in Canada, Abi makes a new friend who shows her that there is a light, even if the deepest darkness. Abi opens her life to the True Light and finds a freedom that she never thought possible. A gentle, moving story, to bring hope to any who struggle with fear. For 9–11s

ISBN 978 0 9536963 6 9

Beech Bank Girls
– Every Girl Has A Story
by Eleanor Watkins

Six teenage friends draw nearer to God and to each other in these fun, moving and honest accounts. Annie, Willow, Rachel, Holly, Amber and Chloe share their laughter, their tears, their hopes, their fears and their secrets with each other and with us. Miracle and party included! Christian chick lit for ages 10–14

> "Really enjoyed it and found it helpful
> at the same time." – Claire

ISBN 978 0 9536963 4 5

London's Gone
by J. M. Evans

London has been bombed by terrorists. Maria watched in horror as the smoke rose from the direction of London. Now she must make a hazardous journey to safety with her sister and a Christian friend, but is anywhere safe now? For Maria, the journey is also inside herself as she begins to discover a side to life that she did not know existed. A thrilling drama full of suspense. For ages 12+

"I just couldn't put this book down!" – Jilly

ISBN 978 0 9536963 2 1

The Treasure Hunt
by J. M. Evans

Ravi, Debbie, Joel and Lance's first exciting mystery adventure. Who is in the back of the white lorry and why are they there? Prayer, faith and their Bible knowledge all help, but when the case takes an unexpected turn, the friends also need to be courageous and obedient. Will they find out what is going on and find the real treasure? For ages 8–11

"The best book I've ever read!" – Emily

ISBN 978 0 9536963 1 4

Mystery in the Snow
by J. M. Evans

Not long after solving their first mystery (*The Treasure Hunt*), Ravi, Debbie, Lance and Joel find themselves with another problem; Ravi's shed has been burgled. Can they find out who did it? The plot thickens as an old lady's handbag goes missing, then a cat disappears. Can all these things be connected? Join the Christian friends as they find answers in unexpected places. For ages 8–11

"So exciting that I couldn't put it down!" – Lydia

ISBN 978 0 9536963 3 8

Find all these and more at www.dernierpublishing.com. *Also available from your local book shop and on-line book store*